Blood and Souls

Blood and Souls

A NOVEL BY

John Davey

N

THE NEPHYRITE PRESS

LONDON

Blood And Souls,
a novel by John Davey.

First published in Great Britain
in 2002 by The Nephyrite Press,
P. O. Box 37815,
London,
SE23 3WQ.

This Woman's Work: Words and Music by Kate Bush
© 1988, Kate Bush Music Ltd., London, WC2H 0QY.
Reproduced by permission of E.M.I. Music Publishing Ltd.

Pigs On The Wing (Parts 1 & 2): Words and Music by George Roger Waters
© 2000, Roger Waters Music Overseas Ltd.,
Warner/Chappell Artemis Music Ltd., London, W6 8BS.
Reproduced by permission of International Music Publications Ltd.

First edition — 1 3 5 7 9 10 8 6 4 2.

A C.I.P. catalogue record for this book
is available from the British Library.

I.S.B.N.: 0-95200-746-0.

Printed in England
by Antony Rowe Ltd.,
Chippenham,
Wiltshire.

Dedicated to Michael Moorcock,
for specific and other inspiration.

BOOK ONE (Beginnings)

Pray God you can cope
I stand outside this woman's work,
This woman's world.
Oh, it's hard on the man
Now his part is over
Now starts the craft of the father.

I know you have a little life in you yet
I know you have a lot of strength left
I should be crying but I just can't let it show
I should be hoping but I can't stop thinking
Of all the things I should've said
That I never said,
All the things we should've done
That we never did,
All the things I should've given
But I didn't
Oh, darling, make it go,
Make it go away.

Kate Bush
This Woman's Work

PROLOGUE (1853 A.D.)

THE DEVIL, SHE noticed, had the most immaculately manicured hands she had ever seen.

This amused her; or, rather, she was amused by the realisation that this one element of His appearance had not actually surprised her.

Everything else about their evening together had, by contrast, been one astonishing revelation after another.

She had certainly not expected the Prince of the Morning to invite her to attend the opera with Him, nor had she anticipated her willingness to accept.

Why, she wondered, had she been so instantly convinced by His simple statement of being whom He claimed? Why had she not feared the implications of His invitation?

It was His eyes, she decided.

In so youthful a face (His appearance suggested an 'age' of around thirty, possibly younger), the eyes — deepest blue; mauve even — moist; not quite tearful — full of infinite intelligence, passion, sorrow — had made her, immediately, so sure.

He had courteously agreed to wait for her to change into something more appropriate for the occasion — He was in full evening attire — and, soon after, she had joined Him in the drawing room; she stood tall in a gown of lilac taffeta and *mousselaine de soie*, trimmed with blonde lace, her long, pale face framed by jet-black hair, worn deliberately and disreputably loose to below her shoulders, much against the fashion of the day.

As it transpired, the opera went virtually unnoticed as they sat in their private box and talked, quietly but incessantly, touching on all manner of subjects. This was possibly the greatest thrill for her. She had long since given up any hope of finding an equal with whom she could converse — was impatient with the women who felt they could not or should not discuss such things; intolerant of the men who found her outspokenness no more than a diverting novelty, who refused to actually listen to anything she said.

Here, with Him, she spoke freely of politics and science and sex and literature, and He seemed genuinely pleased by her remarks and opinions. In turn, He made lively and provocative responses, goading her, almost, to greater degrees of candour.

After the performance — having stood and applauded vigorously, though with no real idea of its worth — they returned by hansom to her apartments and sat, close but not touching, on a chaise longue, once more in the drawing room. Each held a cup of wine, and these were periodically sipped from, in order, it seemed, to detract from the intensity of the moment.

An open fire, prepared by her servants while their mistress was out, flamed high in the grate and danced shadows across the walls. Its light made the wine glow in their hands. She looked into the convex reflection of her face, in her own brightly polished cup, and noticed that her deep blue eyes, seen in this wine-light, now appeared to have taken on a mauvish hue, so like those of the person — the creature, she had to remind herself — sitting beside her.

It had been some time since either of them had spoken.

Eventually the Devil leaned gracefully forward, placed His cup on the floor at His feet, then raised His hands before His face and allowed the fingertips to meet, as if in prayer.

"And your husband, My dear," He said, as if continuing some ongoing conversation. "Where would he be, right now?"

She was taken aback, both by the question and by the fact that she had not once thought of Richard during the whole evening. "Out of the country," she replied simply, "dealing with this Russian situation, or some such. He has no inclination to take me on his travels; I have none to consider where he might be."

"Or with whom?" He enquired, His perfect eyebrows raised.

She inclined her head in affirmation. "Or with whom."

She had risked — and encountered — much ostracism when she married Richard, who was four years her junior, in the belief that a fresher, younger mind would more readily accept her as she was or would like to be. Their courtship seemed to justify this decision but, once wed, he had proved as much a conventional boor as the pompous, withering fools he so admired and she so despised. She actively encouraged his political ambitions now, and turned a blind eye to his philandering, in the knowledge that both would take him away from her for prolonged periods. This, eventually, seemed to suit each of them, especially after her refusal to give him (or any man, she had realised) children.

"Then let's to business," said the Devil, with a smile.

They had not yet discussed the reason for His sudden appearance at her door, and she had not thought to ask. Why not? How much volition had she, over her acquiescence throughout the evening? Was she, even now, under some — quite literally — devilish glamour? She decided she did not care.

As if proof of her suspicions, His next words suggested an ability on His part to read her thoughts. "Why am I here? you might ask. Why indeed? Is it possible you do not remember inviting Me?"

She shook her head, at a loss for words.

"Many people call on Me," He said. "Some do so intentionally. Others — most, perhaps — do not. Sometimes, I will ignore the sincerest plea. At others, I will pay a visit upon the utterer of an offhand oath. I can be an astonishingly whimsical anti-Christ, when I choose to be." He paused, smiling again, as if in appreciation of His own jocularity. "And you? Do you even recall the time when you asked for My assistance?"

This time she nodded. "I do," she said, and the words seemed to echo around her head, like a wedding vow spoken in the most cavernous of cathedrals.

She had called Him. Over and over again she had called Him, though no sounds ever passed her lips. She had lain in bed, just two nights previously, cursing her lot and that of her kind. Her silent cries were tinged with a degree of self-pity, but why should they not be? Despite her best efforts, her future seemed decidedly bleak, with frustration after frustration curbing her every endeavour. She needed, she had realised, that which was denied her.

Power...

That wholly male attribute would, if hers to wield, allow her to achieve all of her goals; all of her dreams. If it was not possible to acquire power because of her gender, she bemoaned, then how else could it be obtained?

Money...

Money overrode all such barriers. Wealth, limitless wealth, would bring her — if not limitless power — at least an ability to influence the lives of those with less. It was a start.

Time...

A lifetime was not enough, she knew, to carry out all she had in mind. Nowhere near enough.

So, she concluded — for power and for money, and for the time to use and enjoy both — why, she would sell her very soul.

To the Devil, she had thought.

To the Devil... To the Devil... To the Devil...

This repeated in her head now, sitting beside Him, as it had then, and she knew why He was here.

"Most people," He continued, "ask only one thing of Me, and consider themselves eternally grateful (if eternally *damned*) —" that smile again — "to receive even a fraction of their request. Those who ask for more invariably get less, if anything at all."

He leaned forward to recover His wine-cup and drained it. When His hands were free again they reached across and clasped one of her own. It was the first time they had touched and a chill shock — neither pleasure nor pain — ran up her arm and across her back, gradually fading along the length of her spine.

He went on, as if nothing untoward had happened: "Eternal life, if that does not seem an overly dramatic term, and eternal wealth — bringing, together, eternal power — is that not too much to ask of Me, do you think?"

"No." Her voice was clear and strong, as if heightened by that strange sensation, the last ripples of which were still dissipating within her.

He seemed to approve.

"How old are you, my dear?" he asked.

"Twenty-nine," she answered, simply.

"You demand so much," He said, "and yet your motives, I feel, appear not to be greed-driven."

"I believe they are not."

Into her mind, then, came flooding images of many people she knew or had known; those she loved, and those she hated. There was her artistic, attractively ugly, over-attentive father, whose features blurred and blended into those of her unimaginative, under-attentive husband. His place was taken by her intelligent, unsophisticated mother, defiantly beautiful, battered and bruised, as so often she was before her violent, untimely death. Old school friends came into view, outnumbered by enemies, old and new. Her one lover before her husband appeared and vanished, all too soon, much as he had done in reality. This jumble of memories threatened to overwhelm her, and she struggled to regain her composure; forced herself to question the reason for these sudden visions. Had the Devil probed her thoughts, reached for her innermost feelings? She tried to close her mind to further delvings, avoided eye-contact, and waited for Him to speak again.

"You fascinate Me —" another smile — "Would you like to know what your future holds?"

She was stunned; had not considered precognition to be among the Devil's skills, then realised she had no right to presume any such thing.

Before she could answer though, He spoke again. "I cannot tell you. I can no more be certain of what will befall you than I can be of My own destiny. Does that surprise you?" Again He did not wait for her to reply. "I see so *many* futures, you understand. So many futures, so many pasts, and not a few presents."

She frowned, and He apologised. "I do not mean to confound you, only to enlighten, but it is hard to explain clearly what one does not fully understand oneself. I see so many possibilities, as I say, but not, by any means, *all*. Only God has total omniscience, though one must surely question his use — or misuse — of it. One's future — anyone's future; yours, Mine, even God's — depends solely upon the decisions one makes. A random choice, or the equally arbitrary alteration of a choice, can mean anything or everything, from instant death to... eternal life.

"I see many futures; both yours, personally, and those of mankind as a whole, and yet none is definite. Man has seen dark ages, and Man has seen golden ages, and all that fall between the two. There are dark futures to be had, and golden futures. Ages which could outshine all others, and ages of nothing more or less than complete and self-inflicted obliteration. I even see, as one possibility, an Age of Women."

Her frown had cleared but, at this, was replaced by a look of defiant, even mocking, incredulity. "I think not," she said grimly.

"And why think you so? Why should that be more or less likely a future than any other? An age in which women gain their (perhaps rightful) place as the governors of Earth. As futures go, I have seen far stranger. Why, at times, I can even foresee futures in which I am inclined to attempt a reconciliation with My maker..." He laughed hollowly and, for the first time that evening and without any real idea why, she shuddered, as He continued, "... but I think not. I am enjoying too much of a fine time the way I am. It would be hard, surely, for Lucifer to give up so many bad habits."

He released her hand, which fell limply into her lap.

"I believe," He went on, "that you will make everything of your future that you desire, and that you will get all that you deserve; but is it, do you think, worth selling your soul for?"

She realised that this was probably her last chance to extract herself from this situation and all it might lead to, and so paused, her breathing shallow and rapid. Again, myriad faces, known and unknown, tried to obscure her vision, but she forced them away, a little more easily than before. Slowly, she looked hard into his purple-tinged eyes, his beautiful face, and said flatly: "Yes."

"Then," He said again, "let's to business.

"I shall bestow upon you the eternal life you so desire. I shall bestow upon you eternal wealth; or, at least, the means by which it can be acquired. Whatever power these gifts might bring is not Mine to bestow, neither can I guarantee its procurement..."

She felt, having committed herself to whatever now befell her, that she had nothing to lose, and so interrupted Him: "And in return?"

His eyes showed the slightest sign of irritation at her question — a brief flicker of deeper redness within the mauve — as if He were annoyed at the break in a well-rehearsed speech. "In return, and foremost, I demand your complete fealty. Nothing less. In addition, I expect something by way of recompense for My generosity." He paused, waited for her to speak, was met with silence and so continued. "You will repay your debt to Me, for all I have done and will do for you, in blood and souls.

"Once a year, every year, for the rest of your eternal life, you must bring about the death of a fellow human being for Me, and you will deliver to Me its corpse. Its blood and its soul are to be Mine. The choice of each subject, however, shall be yours, but you will be denied — though you'll seldom realise it — any already promised either to Myself or to God, and whose purpose for one (or both) of us is as yet unfulfilled. Never fear; there are many whose fate in this respect is undecided. Plenty to choose from, as it were. The methods of their dispatch shall also be yours, and you will be allowed, in time, to discover means by which you can call on My aid when required. Whenever possible, in such instances, I shall assist, or will provide you with a suitable minion in My stead. However, *failure to provide due payment will result in the immediate forfeiture of My gifts to you.* Do you understand?"

"Yes."

"Do you still wish to proceed?"

"Do I have a choice?"

"At this stage, no, I don't believe you do."

"Then let's to business," she said, with a smile which mirrored his own.

"Oh, *indeed*," He said. "Let's." His right hand rose and caressed her cheek. Again she felt the shock reverberate inside her and, for the first time, she felt fear, as He said: "Let's to business. Let us talk of blood and souls, for it is time for yours — your own blood, your own soul — to become My possessions."

His eyes had turned as red as the liquid of which he spoke. The pupils had narrowed to hair's-breadth slits. His hand moved to her throat. She tried to move away from him, but could not, although nothing seemingly restrained her. His fingernails — those immaculate fingernails — touched her flesh and moved downwards, drawing droplets of life-stuff which she felt trickle between her breasts as the nails sliced easily through her laced bodice to expose them.

"Let us talk," He whispered, a voice of pure ice, "of blood and of souls..." Suddenly, he seemed to tower over her. "... And, of course, of *treachery...*"

CHAPTER ONE (Monday)

DAMN THE WOMAN! Simon Colvin yelled, but yelled voicelessly, within the confines of his own head. *Damn her to Hell!*

And then again, he thought, *I love her. I have always loved her. I will always love her.* The words — his conflicting feelings — seemed to be drowned by the noise of an approaching underground train, becoming clear again only after it had halted and then moved on. He should have been aboard one of those departing carriages, but was too involved in his mental turmoil to notice. *How can I love her and hate her at the same time? Why?*

He knew why.

He had betrayed her. He had betrayed her trust, her respect, her love. In one crazy, thoughtless moment, he had lost her. In the arms — *No,* he reminded himself bitterly, *in the body* — of another, his marriage had meant nothing.

Why had he told her? So many of the men he knew had affairs, or flings, call them what they may, or simply got themselves laid occasionally, and none of them told his wife or partner. Colvin, on the other hand, had confessed — felt *impelled* to confess — to Ellie that he had screwed one of his clients, one night after work. He had spent three guilt-racked days trying not to say anything, and had gone nearly insane in the process. What good had it done? Well, it had eased his conscience, at least, but at what price? Ellie had been devastated — totally and utterly.

She had sat and listened to him, too stunned to respond, too saddened to cry. When he had finished; when he sat back, feeling somehow self-absolved, she had simply stood, left the room and gone to bed. He remained downstairs the whole night. Her anger came the next day (*not anger*, he remembered, *fury*). Blind fury replaced the silence, and replaced it with screams; with screams of outrage and injustice and violation. She took scissors to his finest clothes, a hammer to his collection of model soldiers — the two things he was constantly accused of caring more about than her. He simply watched her do it.

When she had finished, she sat down again, just as she had the previous night, in silence. He came and joined her and, passively, she let him take her hand; dark and shaking, enveloped in his; pale, shaking also, but less so. She looked up at him, and there was a pain in her eyes that made his own spring with tears. That was the first time, he realised, that he truly regretted what he had done (*the cheating, or the telling?*).

Now, as another train pulled in which he boarded, only dimly aware of his actions, he recalled her words.

"What did you do?"

He had said nothing, unsure of her meaning.

"What did you to — to her? What did she do to you? I need to know, Simon."

So he told her, as graphically as he felt was... (*what's the word?* he thought now)... prudent. He told her much, but not all. Not for the first time, nor for the last, he failed to give her the truth she deserved.

She sat, as before, and listened. "What did you talk about?"

On safer ground now, he told her that they had simply spoken of trivial things, meaningless things; of their pasts, their presents and their wishes for the future. They had discussed each other's likes and dislikes, and those of their partners. Nothing much. Nothing serious. He stopped suddenly, when he realised that, for the first time, Ellie was weeping.

Even now, nearly a year later, he still could not really understand what she had gone on to say then — how he could have fucked the woman senseless for the rest of his life for all she cared, if only they hadn't exchanged those confidences; those intimacies. Physical betrayal, she said, meant little to her, although it still hurt. Emotional betrayal, however, was different. It was...

He was saved further analysis by the arrival of his train into Victoria (*so soon?*). He rose and left with the surging crowd which carried him tidelike towards the main station concourse. Lost in the noise of others' conversations and the rumble of the escalators, his mind was a blank. He was numb.

Somewhere, as he walked, he heard a familiar tune, played on an unfamiliar instrument; obviously a busker who had not yet been 'moved along'. The song's title, for the moment, eluded him.

When he arrived on the concourse he still glanced up at the large clock and electronic timetable, although he instinctively knew what the time was. As expected, he had some three or four minutes before his train. Suddenly, he realised that he was going to miss it; not that he wouldn't be there when the train was, but that he did not want to get on it. He did not want to go home.

Into his mind, reluctantly almost, came the golden-brown faces of his two children. Sarah was seven, Sam just three. He loved them unreservedly and, until recently, Ellie and he had managed to keep them in ignorance of any 'problems'. Lately though, the common sense that meant arguing only when the children were asleep, at school or maybe playing in the garden seemed to be slipping...

It's a harp, he thought, absently. *How on Earth has a busker managed to get a harp in here?*

He realised he would always go home to see his children, at the same moment that the last whistle blew for his train and he ran for the platform only to watch the rear carriage disappear beyond it. The next train was in ten minutes.

The harp's melody now nagging at him, he thought again of Ellie and how much he needed her. Since that awful day all those months ago, he felt he had done everything he could to regain her... (*her what?*)... her love? He still had that, she told him, in equal measures with her hatred. She insisted that the latter could not exist without the former. She loved him, it seemed, but no longer liked him. That was the easiest — perhaps oversimple — way to describe it, and it was her 'liking' that he missed; that he wanted back, that he begged for.

Nothing seemed to make any difference. He had never seen 'that woman' — the only way either of them referred to his now ex-client

— again. He had changed jobs. He continued to suggest anything he could think of to make amends, but the more desperate he became, the more pathetic he seemed to appear to Ellie, who would now only answer him in response to her full name, Elspeth; this one of the many 'distancing' measures she had begun to adopt.

They had not made love for more than three months and, when they had done so before, it had been far from satisfactory for either of them.

He felt wretched, and she was content to treat him as a wretch.

His one recourse, then, was to fall back on the only way they had ever really resolved anything in their eight years together, since she had flown over from Jamaica to be with him; he did little more, these days, than tell her what he thought she wanted to hear. It did not seem to matter what it was, and whatever it was seldom proved good enough anymore. With his pride shattered, his self-respect in ruins, it meant nothing to him to berate himself in front of her, if that was what a situation appeared to warrant. He was, quite simply, desperate.

The harp seemed all around him now, as he stood at the platform's edge, transfixed by the rails, imagining he could see his face reflected in them. It was a haggard face that he saw, sad and tired, seeming much older than its twenty-nine years, unfashionably bespectacled, crowned by a mop of unruly gingerish hair that was prematurely greying.

He could so easily just let himself fall forward, to fry on the live rail or else get splattered by the next train. Who would care? *Now the self-pity*, he thought. *You sad bastard*. He knew the routine so well; went through it daily, almost hourly. *Damn you, Ellie Colvin! I love you so much, but damn you to Hell!*

He could not jump. He knew that, too. Smiling grimly, he realised he couldn't do it to his fellow commuters; couldn't disrupt their journeys home. He knew he could not jump, but felt that if he could contemplate the very idea then he was about as low as he could ever get. *How much more of this can I take?* It hurt so. *Oh, darling, make it go…*

"Get out of the way, fool!" A bowler-hatted man pushed roughly past, briefcase and umbrella flailing in all directions as he headed for some self-designated spot on the platform. Startled out of his despondent reverie, Colvin glanced up, as his next train drew in to the station, then up further still as the source of the harp became focused sharply for the first time.

Now I am going mad! he said to himself. *I'm standing here at Victoria Station, missing my train, not committing suicide, and watching an angel in the rafters playing Led Zeppelin's* Whole Lotta Love *on a harp.*

CHAPTER TWO (The Nutter On The Train)

REGINALD WATKINS — REG to his few friends — stepped briskly up to *his* door of *his* train and climbed into *his* carriage. He turned quickly and looked back out of the window to make sure the idiot he'd had to push aside just now was not also boarding. No. He was gazing up at nothing at all, like some nutter, but at least he would not be tonight's.

Nutters. They were everywhere, and there was *always* one on every train. Guaranteed. In fact, the spotting and long-distance enjoyment of them was something that, over the years, Reginald Watkins had turned into an art form.

His attention moved back to the carriage's interior, and he made an initial scan of his fellow passengers. No obvious nutters at first glance. They were so easy to spot — drunks, mostly — and seemed to become easier as time went on. Whether this was due to a honing of Watkins's self-proclaimed 'divining powers', or simply a result of the government-induced increase in nutters on the streets (and, consequently, on public transport) — 'care in the community', they had called it — he neither knew nor cared.

All that mattered was the pleasure he derived, every morning and every evening, from being able to recognise his trip's resident nutter, plant himself a discreet and secure distance away whilst retaining an adequate view, and witness the ritual humiliation of some unsuspecting fall-guy or, more frequently, -girl.

It — quite literally — made his day.

A closer inspection failed to reveal any likely candidates. Was this going to be one of those very rare occasions when no 'in-flight entertainment' was on offer? He hoped not. There were still a few empty seats, and so a nutter might yet arrive. Fidgeting slightly with the bowler hat on his lap, he took a sweeping overview of those already seated, pigeonholing each one into a category of his choosing, secure in the knowledge that he was never, *ever* wrong. His 'talent' for reading people so accurately had, he felt, held him in good stead throughout his life and, particularly, in his career in the City. Would it have made any difference if he had known that he possessed no such talent? Would he have believed that, because of this one trait of self-assured presumption, he had been turned down, without even knowing he had been considered, however fleetingly, for more and greater promotions than his petty little mind could ever have thought possible? Would such knowledge have kept him alive through the next twenty-four hours?

Thirty minutes later, and already three-quarters of the way through his London *Evening Standard*, Reginald Watkins had resigned himself to the prospect of an unrewarding journey home.

Finding the article he was currently partway through a trifle dull, he glanced idly over the top of his paper, firstly out of the window to his left and then at his immediate 'neighbours'. Next to him sat a young man, sporting a brand new three-piece business suit and briefcase, hanging eagerly on every word of the middle-aged gentleman to *his* right who, on the rare occasions that the youth was allowed to speak at all, had the intensely irritating habit of anticipating and finishing in harmony each of the poor lad's sentences; seemingly showing interest whilst actually paying scant attention. In turn, this pompous corporate mentor uttered nothing but the official company line — that of an obviously well-established firm — and it was no wonder to Watkins that any glimpse of youthful innovation was so thoroughly and constantly stifled in that archaic leviathan which called itself 'the City'. All the technological advances in the world — all the computers and super-highways and multinational video-conferences — could not rid it of a refusal to drag its sad, withering bulk into anything even vaguely prepared for the demands of a newly arrived twenty-first century. Strangely, Watkins saw no similarity between the substance of the conversation taking place next to him and his own unconscious efforts to perpetuate the very régime he believed he despised.

A glance opposite — reading left-to-right — showed a spotty, sulking little prick with torn, dirty denims and a personal stereo clamped around his ears in sufficiently loose a manner as to allow the constant, tinny rhythm of whatever garbage passed for music these days to escape. Oblivious of the irritation his presence — let alone his music — caused in the carriage, the lad continued to stare vacuously out of the window, probably planning how to evade the ticket inspector at whichever slum's station was his destination, having no doubt avoided buying a ticket at his starting point.

To the yob's left, an elderly, white-haired woman sat huddled over a small black clutch-bag on her lap, apparently asleep. Then, as if his observation of her was a cue, she raised her head slightly, took some knitting from the bag and began wielding a couple of long needles between the loops of some scarlet wool, the end of which trailed back whence it came. The clitter-clatter of her motions seemed at first to keep rhythm, and then to clash unduly, with the cymbalistic din at her side and the rattle of the train's wheels over the tracks' points beyond the window. She looked up suddenly, and straight at Watkins who was astonished to see that she was not just old, but positively ancient. Wrinkle upon wrinkle seemed to fall down her face in folds, out of which shone two surprisingly bright and alert eyes. He could not begin to guess at her age and, to be honest, hoped never to live long enough to end up looking that repugnant. Those intelligent orbs belied their decrepit surroundings, and showed, at least, that the old dear's faculties had not gone the sorry way of the rest of her.

He glanced quickly to the crone's other side; anxious, as always, to avoid direct eye-contact with anyone. His gaze fell on a far friendlier visage, that of a young, blonde girl in her mid-twenties. Immediately, and out of habit, he glanced down at her apparel and noted with pleasure her shortish, if rather prim, business skirt. With practised ease, he shifted slightly in his seat, sliding down a little so as to gain an optimum view of her legs above the knee. Though hardly splayed, they were parted just adequately to allow him to peek discreetly at an exposed portion of inner thigh, to lick his lips involuntarily, and to imagine the rest.

This was another delight provided by the public transport system, and one which rivalled, almost, the entertainment value of its never-ending supply of nutters. Many a happy platform crush had been spent with an out-turned palm pressing surreptitiously against a stray buttock; an arm brushing casually across a protruding breast; his excitement heightened by the recipients' apparent unawareness of his illicit touch.

Nonchalantly he took in the colour and texture of this girl's hosiery, imagining his hand rubbing up and down — unaware that he had begun caressing the bowler on his lap — up and down, each stroke reaching higher and higher until... *Damn it!*

He had not even noticed the train stopping at a station until the girl rose abruptly, grabbed an attaché case from the overhead rack and disembarked. *Damn it! Damn it! Damn it!*

Irritably, Watkins wiped at the steamed glass of the window, glared out and noticed that he was just one stop from his own destination, less than ten minutes away from another interminable evening with his intolerable wife. Nothing was guaranteed to quell his so-recently rising lust more rapidly than the thought of Molly and yet another of her overcooked, underseasoned culinary disasters.

Returning his attention to the carriage's occupants, a glimmer of hope rose quickly inside Watkins as he noticed one of the most recent boarders — a prime nutter if ever there was one. Moon-faced, mumbling, toting a bottle-sized brown paper bag, and with an odour discernible even across the distance that separated them, the tramp sat down some ten or fifteen feet away and immediately struck up an incomprehensible, one-way conversation with a woman who clutched protectively at her small child.

This was it! At last, and so unexpected this late in the journey. The object of Watkins's now waning desire was shed instantly from his mind and he settled down for a session — albeit a brief one — of sheer, unadulterated enjoyment. *Oh, bliss...*

It took him some time, at first, to notice the pricking sensation in his knee. Finally, distracted, he turned to its source and discovered a knitting needle being tapped up and down on him.

"You're going to die, you know."

He returned his gaze to his nutter and tried to ignore the incessant prodding.

"I said, you are going to die. Oh, yes you are. Oh, yes."

"*Madam*," he responded, his voice as righteously indignant as he could make it, "we are *all* going to die. *Some*, it appears, much sooner than others."

He could not believe it! Never, in thirty-five years of commuting, had he, personally, been 'nuttered'. *The shame of it!* Even now he could feel the grins of his fellows bearing down on him; was certain he would find no allies here, no respite. Without looking he just knew that even the drunk had stopped to watch his humiliation. He tried not to squirm physically, and decided to ride out this torment with something approaching dignity.

"You're going to die," said the old woman, once again, "and it will be tonight."

He looked at her repulsively ancient face, into those sharp — mauve, he noticed now: *mauve?* — eyes, and adopted what he hoped was an appropriately bored but disgusted pose, determined to ignore anything she said.

"You're going to die. Oh, yes you are. You're going to die. Oh, yes you are. You're going to die. Oh, yes you are..." She chanted away at him, an obscene litany in a deceptively sing-song tone. "And," she added, "I haven't decided how yet."

"*You* haven't decided how yet?" He rose to the bait. "*You* are going to murder me! Is that it?" He attempted a sneer and failed.

"Oh, no. Not I, no. I haven't decided who, or perhaps even what, is going to send you on your way. I have yet to make up my mind. But rest assured, Reginald Watkins — while you still can — that you'll not see another day. You'll never revel in another poor soul's misfortune; never press another of your feeble erections against some unsuspecting innocent. Never again. You are going to die and, I promise you, your death will not be a pleasant one."

"You'll... You'll..." he stammered, totally lost for words, utterly outraged. "You'll..." He felt self-control flood from him and was as furious at this as he was at the madwoman opposite him. He stood and loomed over her, as if poised to strike out, but she simply stared back at his reddening face; her own chillingly calm and composed.

Fortunately he was saved further embarrassment by the arrival of the train at his station. Still fuming, and for the want of anything better to do, he pathetically knocked the woman's knitting to the floor of the carriage before storming out of the door and along the platform.

As the train began gradually to move again, the old lady gave no indication of noticing the bang of an umbrella on the window from outside as it drew level with Watkins and he yelled some unintelligible profanity at her. Instead, and as if nothing untoward had happened, she bent to retrieve her knitting, relooped a dropped stitch and continued to weave her scarlet web.

Defeated once again, Reginald Watkins went home to die.

Reminiscence (1)

S HE SITS, AND she waits. The room in which she waits is virtually bare — just the chair she sits upon and a small, almost featureless table. Neither of the doors opposite her has opened since she arrived.

She shuts her eyes, and she remembers.

She remembered the very moment that the Devil took her soul. It was the second that He entered her, ice-cold and hard. Brutal.

At that instant, as pain flared through her body and mind, she felt her very soul ripped out of her, drawn from her violated womb.

Her one thought, through all this: *Make it go away.*

She could not move, although it was neither fear nor desire that bound her. She was held down, held open, by some unseen force. The Devil, it seemed, took no chances.

(In the years since then, she had met so many, too many, victims of 'ordinary', mortal rape — *ordinary?* — and their stories, ultimately, differed little from hers. All had felt so totally ruined; all had experienced that same instant of soul-wrenching terror. She wondered, at times, if she, in the end, had not simply been another ordinary victim, the prey of some elaborate, enigmatic charlatan. Then she would look at herself in a mirror, and know better…)

When it was over, when He had withdrawn Himself from His use of her, He had laughed.

Then He was silent.

She lay there, numb, still powerless to move, and watched Him lean down to pick up His wine-cup again. Finding it empty He returned it to the floor and stood, walking leisurely around the room's perimeter, as a casual buyer might at an auction's preview, stroking the contours of a portrait's gilt frame by the door, fingering the golden traceries within a lapis lazuli obelisk on the mantle, for all the world like a longtime and familiar friend from whom formality was no longer expected.

He stopped and examined intently a tall candlestick which seemed æsthetically out of place with the other ornaments in the room. It was of a roughly worked, dull metal, and was raggedly spiked all around its wide, candle-less head. Looking at her for the first time since standing, the Devil raised a quizzical eyebrow, as if aware of and sharing her belief that the object's presence there was in bad taste. Her husband had brought it back from one of his trips abroad — Africa, she recalled — and insisted that it was kept on display, in spite (or perhaps because) of her hatred of it.

Slowly, sensation began returning to her limbs. She felt the heat of the open fire but it failed to quell the shivering that seemed to stem from a tense knot in the pit of her stomach. Mentally, detachedly, she explored her body. It ached, but appeared otherwise unharmed. No fluids flowed from her, of any kind, neither His nor her own. She felt empty, not full.

She began trying to convince herself that it never happened, but another glance at the figure across the room told her it had…

"Let us talk," He had said. His Arctic-chill voice still sighed in her ears. "Of blood and of souls…" Then He had stood, towering over her. "… And, of course, of *treachery*…"

Had raping her been what He had meant? Had that been His treachery? Or was there more to come?

Flashes of His earlier words kept returning to her. "Let us talk of blood and souls. For it is time for yours — your own blood, your own soul — to become My possessions."

She realised, then, that His taking of her was not the treachery He had meant. So…

"Why?"

She realised she had said the word aloud only when He turned again to face her.

His expression seemed as controlled as ever, but His voice betrayed unfamiliar emotion. "It's — it is *expected* of me…"

"*Why?*" she asked again, almost pleading.

"I don't…" His eyes closed briefly, then opened — once more, she noticed, their original colour. "I am sorry."

This she had not expected. "Sorry?" Her voice was full of new-found scorn. "You're *sorry?*"

"Sorry. Yes. Does that surprise you?" His lips curled into a ghost of one of His earlier smiles. "It surprises me."

Gingerly she sat up, gathering her torn clothing around her as best she could. She still felt weak and hollow. She wondered, vaguely, now that her soul was His, whether that emptiness would ever leave her.

He came and sat by her side again, and reached for her hand. She had not meant to flinch but did so anyway, shuffling back, then, just beyond his grasp.

"An eternity of women have been mine," He said, "and very few by choice.

"You ask 'why?'. So do I. But *I* ask why I should feel the way I do now? Why, for the first time since Creation, I should regret an action?

"You are different, and I do not know why that is, either. Will I know? Am I…"

"What now?" she interrupted Him.

"What…" He seemed thoroughly unsure of Himself for the first time that evening, perhaps ever. His face clouded. He frowned.

"I said, what now?"

He took one deep breath and then appeared to relax, again assuming an almost businesslike manner. "You expect more?"

"Of course," she stated boldly — far bolder than she felt — and sat as upright as her aching body would allow. "The Devil, by His own admission, by His very nature, is a treacherous beast. *The* treacherous Beast. I await His treachery. It is, surely, still to come. Rape, after all, is merely rape."

(Those words rang untrue to her then, and had done so, always, thereafter. Rape was a death; a death one had to live with. Those 'ordinary' victims had only one advantage over her. Their mortality brought them hope. Whatever their experiences, their souls were still their own, as were their lives — to mend, hopefully, in time — to heal.)

29

What am I doing? she remembered thinking. *Here I am, talking to the Devil, playing word-games with a creature who has just* — she fought for a word — *defiled me. What on Earth am I doing?*

Again, as she had occasionally throughout that evening, she wondered if she had ever had a choice; wondered just how much influence was being exerted to keep her there; to keep her sane?

"Yes," He said finally. "There is more. Though if it were within my power, which it is not, I would reverse all we have done here tonight. All." He attempted another smile, once more only a shadow of its former glory, and then He continued:

"Treachery is indeed expected of me, is it not? A person calls to me — comes to me sometimes, or I go to them — and, if I choose to, I grant them their desires. However, as you say, by my very nature, I must betray them; as, now, I must betray you.

"My treacheries are always subtle. I never simply promise, and then refuse. I promise, I bestow, and then I — I *warp*. I take an element of my gift, and I turn it against its recipient. I am, after all, the Devil. Fairness is not amongst my attributes. I always — because I have to — make those who call on me regret their decision.

"It is not, I promise you, my choice to do this. It is, I say again, expected of me." He seemed insistent that she should believe Him, but she said nothing, indicated nothing, felt nothing. She sat, and she listened.

"Riches, you asked me for. Riches and power, and eternal life. Is that not so?"

Almost imperceptibly, she nodded.

"All these I have promised you. All these you shall have. Eternal life shall be yours to enjoy, or to endure. Eternal life I shall give you, but not, I am afraid, eternal *youth*.

"You are a remarkable woman; a beautiful, young woman. You believed, no doubt, that your *eternal* beauty would help bring much of what you seek. Therefore, it is that which I must refuse you. You will grow old, and older still, but you will never die. Your flesh, your bones, your organs; all these will age with you. They will be allowed to falter, but never to fail.

"Death will be denied you. Attempt it yourself, seek it from others, and all you will achieve is a greater decline in or disfigurement of your precious beauty, whatever might remain of it at the time.

"I must remind you, also, of your debt to me. Once a year you will bring about the death of a fellow human being. Its blood and its soul are to be mine. You will not have to physically hand it over. Its very demise will suffice as payment. I will know it has been made. And I *must* reiterate these things, for they are crucial to our bargain. The choice of each subject shall be yours. You will be denied, however, any creature already promised either to myself or to God, though you will never realise that such an intervention has taken place. The method of each victim's dispatch shall also be yours. In time you will discover means by which you can use others to do your bidding. It need not always be you who sends them on their way. You can even call on my aid, when required. If, in such instances, I cannot come to you myself, I will provide a suitable minion in my stead."

His voice was growing still stronger, now, no longer so regretful; more self-assured, comfortable with words spoken time and time again over millennia. "Failure on your part to provide due payment will result in the immediate forfeiture of my — My gifts to you. Even that, though, would not bring about the end you will no doubt come to crave. It will merely deliver you to Me — to Hell — and trust Me when I tell you: living a hell on Earth is far, far preferable to the real thing."

She looked deep into His eyes then, and she believed.

Tears brimmed in her own eyes, obscured her vision. She blinked to clear them and, when she looked again, He was gone.

It would be a very long time before she ever cried again.

✳   ✳   ✳

She sits, and she waits. In her lap is a small black clutch-bag. Her hands grip it tightly.

She opens her eyes briefly, shuts them again, and remembers.

She remembered her most recent – she believed her last — 'payment'.

She had left the train at the next station, crossed the bridge to the northbound platform and caught another back towards London, where she returned to her Eaton Square apartments.

There she readied herself for the death of Reginald Watkins.

The Summoning was not an overly complex one, but it did require a great deal of preliminary preparation. Certain artefacts and substances were required to be combined, together with runes of a nature (or supernature) she had not called upon for some time. It pleased her to vary her methods each time. It was one of the few pleasures she could still experience.

When all was set, she closed her mind to much, and yet opened it to much more. She reached out beyond herself, beyond the room in which she stood, beyond the Earth itself, and she spoke.

It began as a whisper; a light, sibilant crooning that barely left her lips. Gradually, as the minutes and then the hours passed, it grew and grew until it seemed, finally, to fill the room, the world, the entire universe.

"Blood and souls," she cried. "Blood and souls for my Lord Lucifer!"

The air around her appeared to moan back, wordlessly, threatening to drown out her own desperate shouts. Through closed eyes she could see smoky shapes writhe in the corners of the room, ectoplasmic tendrils which spread out and reached her, touched her, caressed her.

Again. *"Blood and souls, my Lord! Blood and souls if you will aid me now!"*

She felt a semi-formed presence appear in the room, beside her. It was not Him. She had not expected it to be. With the last of her energies she turned to it, and opened her eyes to behold its hideous visage.

"Go!" she shrieked, straining to hear her own voice over the growing turmoil. *"Do my bidding! Dispatch the one I direct you to! Go!"* Mentally, she focused all of her terrifying powers on one place, many miles away; on one being. She felt the presence next to her grow in size, but not in mass, as it dispersed its shape throughout the room and, at last, disappeared. All noise faded with it. Exhausted, she fell to the floor, panting and faint...

... and Reginald Watkins died.

CHAPTER THREE (Tuesday)

SIMON COLVIN HAD spent much of the previous evening trying to convince himself that it was not even possible to play *Whole Lotta Love* on a harp.

He had failed.

Try as he might, he could not rid himself of the image of that angel, hovering incongruously, not to mention ridiculously — all flowing white robes and golden wings — amongst the ornate ironwork crossbeams of Victoria's roof supports, and staring straight at him with those stunningly bright blue eyes.

He had eventually put his 'vision' down to last night's overtiredness, morbidity and mock-suicidal thoughts, but not before acting sufficiently withdrawn to incur the stony-faced wrath of his wife, Elspeth, who had stormed off to bed at around nine-thirty.

Business as usual…

Now he stood again on that same platform. No harps this time. No music at all. No hallucinations. Business as usual.

He looked down at the rails and remembered being transfixed by them as he had weighed up who would care if he were to live or die. Maybe he had simply needed to invent himself a guardian angel in order to back out of something he had no intention of going through with in the first place.

Maybe.

He looked around now, at the various advertisements and posters, and his attention was held by one in particular, not because of its content — it was for a little-known album by a little-known band — but because of the graffiti scrawled across it. Someone had written, in a none too steady, alternating red-and-black felt-tipped hand, the words FUCKING SUCKARSE NIGGER JEW. Well, it was inventive, he had to admit, although none of it seemed relevant to the picture it adorned. The wielder of the felt-tipped pens, he decided, was *seriously* pissed off, but at what, or with whom, he had no idea. He concluded, resignedly, that however miserable he felt, there was always someone worse off than him. This, however, brought only negligible comfort.

A train was coming in. A sudden push from behind made him rock forwards, almost overbalancing to topple into an oblivion he still had no real desire to sample. His arms windmilled briefly before he stepped back onto a roughly even keel, turned to see an old lady weaving up the platform to his right, and could not believe that her slight frame could have shoved him so hard, especially inadvertently as it had obviously been. He shrugged. One got used to such jostling as a commuter. One had to. (*The ol' five-thirty bump 'n' grind.*)

Somewhat shaken nevertheless, but otherwise unharmed, he took another few small steps backwards, away from the platform's edge, and took the late edition *Evening Standard* from his overcoat's pocket as the train drew to a halt in front of him. Like many others around him, he knew exactly where to stand; not only to be directly opposite a door of his chosen train, but also to arrive opposite the ticket barrier of his home station. The achievement of this feat each evening may have been a small victory — petty, even — but it somehow seemed an important one.

Allowing the few incoming passengers to disembark first, he boarded and sat on the window side of a double seat, his preferred position. Out of habit, he turned to the back page of his *Standard* and, in order, dismissed the sports headlines as not worth pursuing, realised he could do virtually the whole of the crossword puzzle with his eyes shut, and then mourned the passing of the small STOP PRESS column — an old favourite of his — no longer at the bottom of the page. Settling more comfortably into his seat, he opened the newspaper at random and sought a sufficiently absorbing article in which to lose himself.

"**How to identify London's next 'must live' locations**"? No. "**The dying art of suicide**"? *Definitely* not. "**Holes in roads 'cost London £7m in compensation'**"? Ho hum. "**Mystery of man 'scared to death' in locked room**"? Hmmm…

"… POLICE WERE refusing to speculate today on the mysterious circumstances surrounding the death last night of a south-west London man, found by his wife after locking himself in their bathroom, and apparently 'scared' to death. A police spokesman would not comment on whether the death of Reginald Watkins (54) was being treated as suspicious, but in an exclusive interview with the Evening Standard his wife Molly (52) was in no doubt that her husband had not died of natural causes.

She said: 'He came home at the normal time, but was very jumpy and didn't eat his dinner. He went straight to the bathroom, locked the door and refused to come out. Then at about ten o'clock he started screaming, and banging at the door. I tried, but couldn't break it down. Eventually I got one of our neighbours to help me, but by the time we got the door open Reg was dead, and his face was, well, just scared. He'd torn at it with his nails and was all bloody'…"

Bored by this time, Colvin turned the page again. "**Champagne for women stunt pops the cork on frothy old debate**"? Incomprehensible. Sighing, he gave up, closed his paper and his eyes, aware that he daren't doze for fear of missing his station, and rested his head against the coolness of the metal window frame.

It took him some time, at first, to notice the pricking sensation in his knee. Finally, distracted, he turned to its source, and saw a young man, who could only be described as nothing less than beautiful (despite his somewhat dishevelled apparel), poking at him with what seemed to be the sharper end of a guitar's plectrum.

"Hey, man," the youth said to Colvin in a strangely affected voice, as if a mixture of formal introduction and comradely greeting. "How's tricks?"

"I'm sorry," said Colvin, "do I know you?" With an effort to quell certain unfamiliar, not to mention unwanted, sensations in himself, he stared straight into the other's face and immediately noticed the stunningly bright blue eyes. He had seen eyes just like those recently. *Where?* The youth — 'man' definitely seemed the wrong word — had long, blond and ringleted hair which flowed across his shoulders and down between the golden wings at his back. His somehow studiedly dirty denim jacket was covered in patches, and…

… *Rewind…*

… Wings? *Wings! Oh, no, no.* Colvin closed his eyes again, tightly shut, and counted to ten.

… *Eight. Nine. Ten. Open.*

"How's tricks, dude?" asked the angel.

"Tricks?"

"Yeah, man, tricks, you know. Tricks. Dig?"

"Dig?"

The conversation was not going well.

"You are Simon Colvin, right?"

Colvin nodded limply, and risked a glance around him to see who else was watching the exchange. No-one seemed to have noticed, or to be moving… at all.

"It's cool, man," said the angel. "These cats an' chicks ain't gonna bother us none. They're chilled."

"Chilled?" He was beginning to sound ridiculous, even to his own ears.

"Yeah, man. Look around you. Look outside."

Colvin peered out of the window and saw that the train had stopped. Another, closer inspection confirmed his worst fears. A line engineer hovered, unmoving, a few inches above the hole he had just finished digging, frozen midway through his leap down into it. A bird in the sky above him hung motionless in the air. A scan around the interior of the carriage again showed no signs of life, in anyone, anywhere.

"You've… you've stopped time?" he asked, dimly aware of the ludicrousness of the question, the very impossibility of its recipient.

"No, man. Even *I* can't do that. I've just… slowed it down a little. Well, quite a lot, actually. Pretty neat, huh? *Trippin'.*"

"Trip…" Colvin stopped himself, mid-echo, and resolved to try and come to terms with — get on top of — this bizarre situation. "Who *are* you?"

"Name's Dylan," said the angel.

Keep a grip, Simon. "Someone Dylan? Dylan Someone?" He had aimed for nonchalance, but missed.

"Just Dylan."

"I see." *Oh, well. In for a penny…* "You don't by any chance own a harp, do you?"

"Did. Swapped it for an axe, dude. A Strat, twelve-string custom job. Psychedelic lacquer finish; the works."

Much relieved to discover that they were discussing guitars, and not tree-felling weaponry, Colvin relaxed… a little.

The angel, Dylan, repeated his earlier question: "You are Simon Colvin, right?"

"*Who the hell are you?*" Colvin yelled.

"Cool it, man, I'm an angel. I'm Dylan. I'm *your* angel."

"My…"

"Your angel, man, tuned in to your every vibe. You know… Ziggy played guitar. Suzanne takes your hand. Fast and bulbous. Bismillah! Somebody called me Sebastian…"

Wondering if they were still speaking the same language, Colvin could only utter, "I thought you said your name was Dylan…"

"It is, man. Dylan. Isle o' Wight, you know."

"Then who's Sebastian?"

It was the angel's turn, now, to look puzzled, uncertain. He mumbled something under his breath, and then continued: "Hendrix? Woodstock?"

"I'm sorry," said Colvin, realisation slowly dawning on him, "are we talking about music?"

"Sure, man!" Dylan seemed much relieved. "Woodstock, dude. I was there!"

"*You* were at Woodstock?" The youth could not possibly have been more than eighteen, maybe twenty years old.

"Sure. A whole tribe of us went, travelled up from Oxford."

"Oxford, Maryland?"

37

Puzzlement again. "No, Oxford, Oxfordshire, man. Well, Witney, actually, just outside the city. Took the A4095 up to Woodstock…" He still seemed in need of reassurance. "Woodstock, dude! *Woodstock*. You know. Hendrix. Cream. Joplin. Take That. Sha Na Na. Lute Train. Creedence…" Maybe it was the look on Colvin's face, but the angel's began to display a distinct level of self-doubt now. "Man, you had to have been there. Max Hutchinson's farm. It was *trippin'*…"

"Yasgur's."

"I beg your pardon…"

"Dylan, Woodstock's in New York." Colvin found himself relaxing, despite the outlandishness of the situation, enjoying the other's obvious discomfort.

"New York?"

"As in New York, America."

"It *is*?"

"It is."

"Shit, man, I knew that research department had screwed up. They swore to me. 'Simon Colvin', they said. 'Music freak', they said. 'Mention Woodstock', they said. Gave me all the key words an' everything. Aw, fuck it, man! Listen, can I drop all this hippy crap now?"

Colvin could not resist a somewhat wicked, self-satisfied smile. "Please do," he said, and then added, "You said 'research department'?"

"Yes, that's right." Colvin noticed immediately that Dylan's voice had changed to something… well, something more in keeping with his beauty. Soft, but strong (*like all good toilet tissue*) and perfectly modulated. A voice you could trust; could fall in love with, even. "You had to be checked out, researched, to make sure you were the right one for the job, and we needed to know the best way to make contact; to make you believe. 'Music', they told me. I guess they were wrong…"

"Well, you're not wrong. I do like music. I'm no 'freak', but I know what I like. It's not that. It's just that your facts were… well, a little awry. What job?"

"Job?"

"You said you had to make sure I was the right one for the job."

"I said that?"

"You said that."

Dylan sighed despondently. "I *told* them they should have sent someone more qualified. They wouldn't listen. They never do."

"Who doesn't?" Colvin was not at all sure he wanted to hear the answer; still wasn't sure he was even having this conversation. Had he finally lost it, big time? He was saved any answer he might have feared by Dylan's change of subject.

"Listen, Simon, I need to take you somewhere. I need you to come with me. I need you to trust me. Okay?"

"Where are we going?"

"Heaven."

CHAPTER FOUR (One Man's Heaven)

"A M I DEAD?" It seemed the only thing to say.
"No, Simon. You're not dead."
"Will I be?"
"No."

"Then..." He knew there must be a question he should ask — hundreds, thousands of them — but none would come. An hour or so ago he was sitting at his desk, poring over columns of figures. Now... here he was, on a train frozen in time, talking to an angel about going to Heaven. (*Trippin'*.)

"Dylan. That *is* still your name, isn't it... Dylan?"
"Yes."

"Well, Dylan, I'm kind of at a loss to know what to say. This is all a little... odd, to me. Do you know what I mean? I mean... what the fuck do I mean? I don't know. Am I mad? Insane? Shit..." He closed his eyes again, tried to feel and listen for the movement and rumble of the train beneath him. Nothing. He rubbed his hands roughly over his face. Eventually he reopened his eyes and stared long and hard at the angel sitting opposite him. "Okay," he said. "Tell me."

Dylan's eyes were full of compassion. He said nothing, but his wings twitched a little at his back.

Colvin realised that he could weep, and with ease. He was that close. But he knew that if he began to cry, he would probably never stop.

Finally, Dylan spoke:

"Simon, you are needed for a task. No-one else can do it. It has to be you. I have to take you to meet my — my superiors. They will explain everything to you, as best they can. You must understand, Simon, this has never been done before. No living creature has ever been allowed to go where I am taking you now. You are the first. You will be the last; the only. We need you, Simon."

"*Who* needs me? Why me?"

"I can't explain that. I'm not sure any of us can, really." He grinned a little sheepishly. "The research was done, Simon. It *is* you."

"You'll forgive me if I confess to being a little wary of your researchers' accuracy, Dylan."

"Trust me."

(*eyes blue beauty love man woman old need trust heaven help heaven help us all betray help hell wedding love trust me*) "I do."

"Then close your eyes again."

"Open them."

Colvin did so. No carriage. No train. Just a room. Dylan, by his side. Doors. A table. A chair. His doubts somehow subsided.

Had there been a stairway, pearly gates, Saint Peter, he would have known he was mad; known that he finally had lost it. Big time. This, for some reason, he could believe in.

A door opened and a small, plain-looking woman in her early thirties entered the room. Colvin felt a subtle warmth enter him. A pleasure? An ecstasy? Neither. A warmth. She nodded to him, and then to Dylan. When she spoke, it was like the distant, watery peal of faraway church bells. Pure. Lovely. (*love*) "Dylan, would you be so kind as to fetch another chair for Mr. Colvin, and then you must leave us."

"Yes, ma'am."

"Do please take a seat, Mr. Colvin."

(*trust*) "Simon," he said.

"Simon."

He sat across the table from her. They were alone. She wore a loose-fitting, rather drab robe from which she produced a small ledger. "Our visitor's book. Would you sign in, please."

"But…" He opened the book. It had just one page; no entries. He signed his name, went to date it and then changed his mind.

She closed the book and returned it to her gown. "Thank you. Some of us here are sticklers for such things. It keeps them happy." She smiled. (*heaven*) "Do you know where you are, Mr. Colv… Simon?"

"Heaven?"

"Not quite. Heaven is through that door. We'll go there soon though, together. Do you know why you are here?"

(*help*) "A task?"

"A task. Indeed. Simon, what does the word Armageddon mean to you?"

"A pretty average nineties' Bruce Willis movie…"

She smiled again, showing both tolerance and disapproval; the capacity for infinite amounts of both.

(*woman*) Colvin realised that he did not want this woman's disapproval. He wanted her to love him, to need him. (*need*) "I'm sorry," he said, and he was. A thought occurred to him then. "What is your name?"

This time she seemed genuinely surprised, startled. "My name? I… I have no name."

"Then what should I call you?"

"Anything you wish."

"May I — may I call you Elspeth?" He had no real idea why he asked that.

"I prefer 'Ellie'."

"Are you…?" He frowned.

"No, I am not her, Simon, but you may call me by her name."

"Thank you."

"Shall we go to Heaven together?"

He had no doubts, now. "Yes."

They rose from the table and he walked to her side, where she enfolded her hand around his elbow. It was the first time they had touched and a shock of greater warmth — neither pleasure nor pain — ran up his arm and across his back, gradually fading along the length of his spine. She led him towards the door whence she had entered, and it opened in front of them. They stepped through…

43

... into a corridor. It was long, seemingly and dizzyingly endless, and bright white, though with no obvious means of illumination. To each side of them, stretching for (*eternity?*) as far as the eye could see, were small glass-fronted cubicles, about four feet square with no visible ceilings. In each cubicle was a person, sometimes male, sometimes female. Each sat in a chair not unlike the one Colvin had just vacated. Each bore a serene — a *totally* serene — look upon his or her face. "Heaven," said the woman at his side.

"I must admit, it's not what I expected." He paused. "What *is* it, exactly?"

"Well, first of all, I should explain that what you see here is not a precise representation of Heaven, as such. That reality exists in a dimensional form which your mortal mind would find impossible to comprehend, and so we have adapted it — for *metaphorical* purposes, shall we say? — solely for your benefit." She stopped, seeming to expect a reaction to this, but received none, and so continued: "I suppose the closest thing to it that you could understand is a kind of... Virtual Reality, as you know it. Every resident of Heaven occupies one of these metaphorical 'booths', and each has, to all intents and purposes, everything they could possibly desire. Every man, woman and child here sees, smells, hears, tastes, feels and does all of their favourite things — as many or as few of them as their imaginations can cope with — for eternity, and without boredom. It is Heaven."

"I see." He was not convinced. "Do they know they are in the booths?"

"Oh, no. As far as they are concerned, they are all in a room (or rooms) of their choice, or in a house, a garden, a field, an island, an ocean. Whatever they wish it to be, and with whomever they wish.

"Contrary to popular belief, you see, Heaven is by no means infinite, and there is something of a chronic space shortage here. These booths — in their true form — are an attempt to alleviate that problem. I do assure you, though, that whatever Heaven's residents wish it to be, it is."

"For eternity? Without boredom?" He plainly remained sceptical. "Can they never change their... their environments?"

"We do not know. It is not for us to interfere. Each person's heaven is, and must be, uniquely their own."

"But you created all this."

"No. Those of us whose responsibility it is to oversee the residents here did not create this; do not really understand it, but we do know that it works."

"*How* do you know?" He was insistent.

"Look at their faces, Simon."

He looked, and then he knew that she was right. It *was* Heaven.

As they talked, they were walking along the corridor, past cubicle after cubicle, person after person, face after face, and now they stopped as Colvin peered more intently into the booth of a middle-aged woman to whom they stood closest. He noticed a flickering, a shadow, pass rapidly behind her. Nothing around them nor in the cubicle seemed to cast the shadow, which he saw grow more agitated then subside and disappear. Checking closely, further up and down the corridor, he realised that several of the booths contained these flickering shadows. He had to know, but hesitated before he spoke; before he used the name. "Ellie, what are those?" He pointed.

"Shades," she said, "shades of Hell."

He waited for an explanation. She seemed to be looking for the right words. "If you had opened the other door from that room back there, Simon, it would have taken you to Hell: a corridor, in effect, just like this one, full of people just like these, in every way except for their expressions. One look at their faces would have turned you quite mad.

"There are countless numbers of these booths, you see, in both Heaven and Hell, and each is capable of sustaining an equally vast selection of imaginable environments, as you call them. For every environment, however simple or complex, there are always two potential residents; one for whom it is a heaven, one for whom it is a hell. What you see here is… interference, if you like, as on a television screen, between the residents of two identical environments. Neither seems aware of the other's presence, which is not really a physical presence anyway.

"This is… this is hard to explain in terms you can understand, Simon. In Hell you would see, on occasion, similar shadows in booths there as well. They would not flit about, as these you see here do. They would be still, calm. Nobody here knows why this happens, exactly, but perhaps these crossovers are essential to some sort of balance. Perhaps they are the very thing that avoids the boredom you wonder about. Shall we return?"

He realised that he was reluctant to leave this place, or at least to relinquish the feeling of peace that pervaded every fibre of his being when he looked at the faces around him. Slowly, though, he nodded and felt his eyes close, against his volition. The next thing he knew, he was sitting again in the room, on the chair, at the table, opposite the one — the other one — whom he now called Ellie.

"Simon, are you a religious man?" she asked.

"No, I'm not... I mean... I wasn't. I don't — I don't know. Am I?"

"I am not asking you to be.."

"Well, shouldn't I be, after all that? Isn't that why you showed it to me?"

"Belief is no guarantee of Heaven, Simon, any more than non-belief is a guarantee of Limbo or of Hell. Are you a good man, do you think?"

"I don't know, Ellie. Again, I don't really know. I try to be, I think, but I'm not sure how well I do."

"And, without the levity this time, Simon, what does the word Armageddon mean to you?"

He sighed. "The end of the world, I suppose. A final battle between good and evil. Something like that. It's been a while since Sunday School, I'm afraid. Is that it?"

She smiled. "Well, it originally referred to a place, rather than an event, but that's a close enough approximation for our purposes. For your purposes. For your task. Are you ready?"

Despite not even knowing what he was being asked to be ready for, he realised that this was probably his last chance to extract himself from this situation and all it might lead to, and so paused, his breathing shallow and rapid. Slowly, he looked hard into Ellie's pale green eyes, and said flatly: "Yes."

She, too, paused; seemed further to compose her already quiescent features, and then spoke: "Simon, it seems that Armageddon, as you understand it, is almost upon us. However, the rules, as it were — at least in the way that your Bible and other such histories interpret them — have been changed.

"The event no longer requires a vast conflict, between all the minions of Heaven and Hell, living and dead, but instead a far smaller affair, between two individuals; one representing the forces of good, the other evil.

"This force for evil has already been chosen. She was chosen by Lucifer nearly one hundred and fifty years ago. She lived then, and she lives still, if one can call her existence living. She knows her destiny. However, the force for good is, or perhaps was, wholly unaware until today that he has been chosen." Again she paused.

"You have *got* to be fucking kidding!" said Colvin forcefully, if a lot more calmly than he felt.

"No, Simon, I have never been more serious."

"Me? *Why me?* Why on Earth me, for Christ's sake —" at which she grimaced, but he was not in the mood to notice, nor to apologise had he done so — "I'm just a man. Just one man. I'm not a priest. Not a pope. Nothing! I'm married. I have children. I'm a good father, if a lousy husband. I've screwed around. I've lied. I've cheated. Oh, shit! Shit! Shit! I'm a fucking tax inspector, of all things! What kind of a hero, a 'force for good', is that?"

"Simon..."

"No! Why?"

"Simon..."

"Why me? damn you! Why me...?" He realised that he was shaking, weeping, uncontrollably. *"Why?"* he managed once more, barely a whispered croak. She reached forward and touched her fingertips to his forehead, and again he felt that deep warmth enter and dissipate within him. He calmed.

"Simon," she said, "I do not know why. None of us does. We only know that it has to be. Your actions before this day mean nothing. You are no more or less able to deal with what is to come than any other mortal, and a mortal it must be. You will not be alone, though. Whilst we cannot predict the course the next few months will take, nor what might be expected of you, we can provide you with help and guidance; with assistance..."

"You?"

"No. Not I. Dylan will be with you, whenever you need him. He will help you all he can; as much as any of us can."

He nodded. "It could be worse," he said, and managed a tired grin.

"It will be, believe me. Worse, and harder, than you can even begin to imagine. The woman chosen to fight you has many, many powers at her disposal; long learned and much used. You have none, save those you already possess."

"And they are?" he asked.

"You will know."

"I wish I shared your confidence."

"Do not mistake faith for confidence, Simon. I have faith in you, because I must, but I do not believe you will win. I believe — we all believe — that evil's time to dominate Earth is almost upon us. Anyone who thinks it is already there is sorely mistaken. Hell on Earth *will* come about though, unless you can stop it."

"I thank you, Ellie, for your honesty."

"Honesty is the least that I owe you."

He sighed again, a heavy, long, drained sigh. A few hours ago — a lifetime ago — he was sitting at his desk, poring over columns of figures. Now... "What now?" he asked.

"I do not know, but *you* will. It is agreed that the forces of evil will make the first, the opening move towards Armageddon. You must wait, and you must be ready."

"It's '*agreed*'?"

"Yes. There are, as I say, rules to this thing, though none of us is privileged to know them all."

He should be resisting this, he felt, but lacked the energy. He was tired; too tired to argue. He thought of what could happen to him if he embarked on this madness which, even now, he could not truly believe was about to take place; and then he thought of what would happen to his wife and children if he failed. He knew, now, why he had been shown a glimpse of Heaven. He looked again, deep into Ellie's — *this* Ellie's — eyes, and he believed. "Okay, so what happens next? Right now?"

"We return you to Earth, of course; to London, to your train, to your home and to your family. Do you trust me, Simon?"

"I must."

"Then close your eyes again."

Colvin did so, and then opened them once more… to feel the train moving him along, to hear his fellow passengers' conversations, to see a line engineer leap into the hole he had just finished digging. No room. No doors. No table. No chairs. No angels…

… and Simon Colvin headed home.

REMINISCENCE (2)

S HE SITS, AND she waits. In her lap is a small black clutch-bag. Her hands grip it tightly.

She opens her eyes briefly, shuts them again, and remembers. She had remembered her last. Now she remembers her first.

She remembered waiting until the anniversary of her pact with the Devil, fearing to take the action she knew she must.

It was late, approaching midnight, and Richard was still not home. If he did not return soon, she was uncertain what she would do. All of her plans hinged on his presence. It was to be him. It could be no other, the first. She knew that; had known it for a whole year.

Just then, she heard the key turn in the lock of the front door, and the sound of his feet in the hallway as he divested himself of coat and hat.

There were no servants to wait on him. She had given them the night off, as she had each Friday for the last year, to ensure that nothing would arouse suspicion, Richard's or otherwise.

He had been back in the country for just over a week, something else she had hoped for, not knowing what would happen if he were not in England. They had spoken little, since his return, and much of the time he had been absent from the house. She wondered if some other, supernatural force had perhaps had a hand in his returning, both to the country and to the house this evening, so fortuitously.

She had no doubts — none at all — that the events of a year ago had really taken place. She still had that chill feeling in her womb. Would it remain with her, for all of her (*eternal*) life?

Now she crouched in the dark, in the drawing room, behind the chaise longue, knowing that Richard would stop there first, light a lamp, sit and smoke a cigar before coming up to a bed they did not share.

As predicted, he entered the darkened room and she took a firmer grip on the spiked metal candlestick — the one she so detested — in her slightly perspiring hand. She knew what she had to do, now. She thought she should be trembling, feeling scared... something... but instead an overwhelming calm was upon her, which seemed to direct her every thought and action.

As he bent forward over a low table by the chaise longue, removed the glass from the lamp and lit the wick, she arose and raised her arm, poised to strike. Her first instinct was to hit out there and then, whilst his back was to her, but she stopped herself, paused and spoke: "Richard."

He turned, mild astonishment on his face that she should have been there at all, and in the dark. It was her habit, of late, to retire mid-evening. He seemed not to have noticed her upright arm until it began to swing down towards the side of his head, by which time it was too late.

She was surprised by the noise of the impact, the jarring through her arm as candlestick struck cheekbone and shattered it. His look of astonishment changed to one of deep shock, though he showed no sign of registering the pain he must have known. A small yelp escaped him, as if an inarticulate query, and yet he seemed rooted to the spot. Her arm went back again, at a higher angle this time, and fell onto the crown of his head. She felt the first grip of panic then, as one of the candlestick's spikes buried itself into his skull and lodged there, almost tugging the stick clear out of her hand as he jerked backwards with an automatic spasm bearing no semblance to an attempt at escape. She wrenched the candlestick free, and was sprayed as she did so with blood and brain matter as her pulling toppled his body forward again, towards her own. His arms seemed to grip her around the waist, and gore pumped from his ruined head onto her. She struck again, but was hampered by their respective positions and made no impact. A bubbling noise, and then a wheezing, wet cough, slipped from between his lips, and he slid slowly down her, fell across the chaise longue and rolled onto the floor. She stepped back then, walked around and half-kneeled, half-fell down beside him. His whole body continued to shake, as if in an epileptic fit. She hit him again… and again… and again… and again…

The bath's water had long since gone cold, and was a uniform pink, in which darker patches clotted and eddied as she moved, rocking slowly back and forth.

Eventually, she realised she was shivering, and so stood, stepped out of the tub and let excess water drop onto the bath mat. She grabbed a towel and began to dry herself, still trembling and detachedly watching the colour of the towel change as it soaked up the bloody patina from her skin.

She stood in front of a full-length mirror and stared dispassionately at herself. Her deep blue eyes — as much at odds with her pale skin as her black hair was with both — seemed, for once, lifeless. There had always been a sparkle in them, those eyes. When had it left? Just now? A year ago? She could not remember anything, clearly, that had taken place before repeatedly raising that candlestick, over and over…

When she had first risen from Richard's finally motionless body, she had backed away from it, staring both with horror and a deep fascination at the gory scene before her. The candlestick slipped from her fingers, and fell with a discordant clang to the floor. Jumping at the sound, she looked down at her makeshift weapon, and saw that two of its spikes, from which hung strands of blood-matted hair, were bent out of shape. Yet, as she watched, they had straightened before her eyes. A sudden noise in the direction of Richard's body drew her attention away from this puzzle, and she saw the pool of blood around him begin to bubble and froth; to move like quicksilver across the floor and ooze back into his wounds, the ragged flesh of which moved also, as if in a breeze. A strangled cry escaped her as she turned and fled from the room, terrified that this reanimation would bring the corpse back to life, to wreak its revenge upon her.

Outside in the hallway she ran for the locked door to the basement, gasping for air, shaking, panic threatening to consume her as she fumbled with the stubborn key. After what seemed an eternity she heard the tumblers fall into place and yanked the door aside with a crash, recklessly descending into the gloom below.

As soon as she felt her feet touch the stone of the basement's floor, she made her way blindly towards a glow offered by the furnace, bumping into several unseen obstacles in her path.

Despite the roaring heat, she shivered as she stood close to the furnace, and the sweat on her forehead chilled her further still. Her breathing had slowed though, and she strained to listen for sounds from above. Nothing could be heard beyond the noise of the flames beside her.

Her skin began to itch and, scratching idly at her hand, something seemed to flake away, lodging under her nails, which she realised was heat-dried blood. Richard's blood. Lifting her fingers up, in front of her face, they appeared to be stained black in the radiance from the furnace, and she rubbed them on her gown, only to find more blood there, semi-congealed and sticky.

It was then that she fell to the floor with a cry, and vomited, straining and retching long after there was anything left to expel.

She could not have gauged how long she remained there, on her knees, but the nausea eventually passed, and was replaced with a strange, numbing sense of tranquillity which, in time, gave her the strength to stand.

Fastidiously, yet without revulsion, she removed all of her clothes then, wiped the mess from the floor with them, and hurled them deep into the furnace's belly, watching them burn until there was nothing left to see.

She knew that she was no longer afraid of whatever she would find upstairs — knew somehow that she had no reason to fear — but it was still a long while before she ascended to the hallway. Even then she avoided the drawing room, and dashed past its closed door. Hesitating for just a second or two at the foot of the next flight, she resigned herself to whatever fate was ultimately due to befall her, and continued resolutely up to the bathroom.

Almost two hours later, naked still, but clean, and dried, with the towel and the bath mat hanging loosely in her hands, she descended the stairs again, all the way to the basement, and added them to the flames. Slowly, then, she went back up one flight, standing for some time outside the drawing room, listening intently, hearing nothing. With a deep intake of breath, she re-entered the scene of her crime.

Richard lay, as he had before, between the chaise longue and the low table, but no blood covered his body; there was none on the floor about him, nor on the furniture he had rolled across as he fell. His head no longer bore any signs of the blows she had rained upon it, and the candlestick was back in its place upon the mantle.

He seemed asleep. She stopped, paused, and then spoke: "Richard." No answer.

Staggering forward, she leaned down, feeling for a pulse. There was none. He *was* dead.

Righting herself, she turned and, with a small nod of satisfaction, walked calmly out and back up the stairs once more, to her own bedroom where she dressed in night attire, there to await the arrival in the morning of her servants.

Massive heart failure, the coroner had said; unusual in one so young, but not unprecedented.

The funeral came and went, and with it the sympathetic looks, words and gestures of friends and colleagues. All agreed it was a tragedy. All commented on, to each other, or described to others, the fortitude with which she bore this sad blow, the loss of her beloved husband.

The Last Will and Testament was read.

She was now a very wealthy woman.

✻   ✻   ✻

All this she remembers.

Still she sits. Still she waits…

BOOK TWO (The End Of The Beginning)

If you didn't care what happened to me,
And I didn't care for you,
We would zig zag our way through the boredom and pain,
Occasionally glancing up through the rain,
Wondering which of the buggers to blame
And watching for pigs on the wing

Roger Waters
Pigs On The Wing

Chapter Five (Another Monday)

Simon Colvin sat upon a bench, on his home train station's London-bound platform, awaiting the arrival of the 06:58 to Victoria. That, of course, was dependent on its arriving on time... or at all. Nevertheless, it was one of those very finest of Spring mornings, at the start of the season, with a bright sun rising and beginning to warm the sweet-smelling air; to illuminate the foliage on and around the tracks' embankments.

He sat opposite a poster advertising a new laser-printer's unlikely claim to faithfully reproduce one hundred and twenty-eight million different colours. Looking around him now, he could swear he saw a hundred and twenty-eight million shades of green alone. Nature, it seemed, could always out-produce Man. There was something exceptionally vivid about those short-lived Spring greens (*isn't that a vegetable?*), before the city's grime began to settle on them; before the season's later, hotter sun baked that grime on, and the colours lost their edge for another year.

Today, for the first time in many, many months, it felt truly good to be alive. There was no reason for it; none that he could fathom, anyway.

He could even, without too much effort, persuade himself — or pretend — that he had never been to Heaven, nor conversed with angels, nor been enlisted to fight against ancient evil for the destiny of mankind.

It was no good. No matter how he phrased it, it still sounded ridiculous, not to mention impossible, especially as nothing at all had happened in the weeks since his 'visit' (*visitation?*). No, it did not take a great exertion of will to doubt the whole thing had ever taken place.

He had neither seen nor heard anything from Dylan, or from the woman who claimed to have no name, whom he had chosen (for some reason he still did not fully understand) to call 'Ellie'. Was she, too, an angel, like Dylan? He wasn't sure that she was.

Sitting here now, waiting for his train, everything that had happened seemed like a dream, an hallucination, anything but reality. He had begun to question much of what he had been told in Heaven. He needed answers, or at least reassurance, but had so far had nothing but silence.

It seemed there was no-one who could provide those answers. Not even owning a Bible, he had gone along to his local library a few times, looking up anything that might relate to his situation, but had drawn a blank. The references were all but meaningless to him.

His train approaching, Colvin shook himself out of this reverie, stood, and moved forward to the edge of the platform. Failing to find a seat upon boarding, he remained standing near the door, trying to ignore the cacophony of mobile 'phone conversations that had already struck up around him, staring instead at the passing greenery.

He began to consider the idea of a family outing this coming weekend — a picnic, maybe — into the country, where the golden patchwork quilt of rapeseed fields must be starting to take hold across the farmlands, overseen and punctuated by majestic chains of electricity pylons (*am I the only one who finds them majestic?*) striding towards the horizon.

Of course, they would have to find an area unaffected by the new foot-and-mouth epidemic currently rife in the countryside. There must be somewhere, surely?

Would Elspeth even agree to such a trip? He hoped so. The past weekend had been relatively tolerable for them both, whilst he had kept himself occupied with various household repairs.

Elspeth. Beautiful, moody Elspeth. His wife of eight years. How much longer? he wondered. 'Relatively tolerable' was hardly a healthy basis for future growth. How much longer could they continue hurting each other?

Was it only fear that kept them together? Fear of the unknown. Fear of being alone. Fear…

He was afraid, he knew. Of Elspeth? *Your anger scares me*, he thought. *Your sadness cuts me.* No, not of her.

Realising he was in danger of slipping out of his earlier good mood, into an altogether more familiar, darker one, he focused instead on past, happier times; on the moment he had first set eyes on the woman who was to become his wife.

He had been holidaying alone in Jamaica, relatively cheaply as it was still hurricane season, and was staying at an hotel in Montego Bay, a treat he had been promising himself for several years.

Though never one for sitting by swimming pools, it seemed the only thing to do upon returning from that day's round trip to Kingston. The very cheap tourists' map he had bought at the airport when he arrived had advised him that the capital was one hundred miles from Montego Bay. What it had not told him was the measurement's as-the-crow-flies basis (at best), bearing little semblance to its as-the-car-drives reality. Fortunately, he had set off very early that morning, and Kingston, it turned out, like most capitals, did not have a great deal to recommend it. Deciding against staying overnight in the city, he had taken the same circuitous route back to his hotel and still got there before sundown, where he now sat sipping at a large and well-chilled rum punch.

Having foregone a shower in favour of a couple of lengths of the pool, he allowed the still-warm, last rays of the sun to dry him, and the slight breeze to cool his skin and help erase memories of a less than successful day.

"Um…" That was her first 'word' to him. 'Um'. He looked up and straight into the dying sunlight, still sufficient to temporarily blind him. Silhouetted there, baily's beads shimmering around her head, was a woman whose features he completely failed to make out. He squinted, his hand to his brow, but could focus on nothing.

"You're on my towel," she said, dropping to a discreet crouch having recognised his impairment. A simple blink of the eyes clarified his vision, and there she was. He loved her.

Prior to that point in his life, he would have sworn that so-called love at first sight was a fallacy, one dreamed up by authors and screenwriters, and yet from that moment they had been inseparable. (He had, indeed, been sitting on Elspeth's towel, having returned to the wrong deckchair after his swim.) The rest of his holiday was tinged with precisely the sort of ickiness that Hollywood seemed to take pride in, and which would have turned his stomach had it been described as happening to another. A week later, they had parted in tears at Sangster airport, as she arranged to join him in England within the month. A month after that, they were married. Seven months later, Sarah was born. Everything was perfect.

Seven years later, nothing was perfect.

Taking the opportunity to stand without holding on to anything, as the train was at a station, he removed a dog-eared photograph of Elspeth from his jacket's inside pocket. He had had it laminated for extra protection, but it still bore the signs of a great many viewings. It had been taken during that holiday, the day after they first met, in her home village in the foothills of low mountains close to Montego Bay. She was smiling; a smile which, to this day, could still melt him, though it was now so rarely seen. Likewise, her thrilling, tinkling laughter, always a joy to hear, was a thing of the past, as was much else. He looked at her small, almost perfectly round face, into her dark, all but black eyes, and sighed.

The hand that held this cherished photograph shook a little, which he put down to the train's renewed motion, as an earlier question came back to nag at him: how much longer? How much longer could they continue hurting each other? He really did not know. Love, it seemed, was no longer enough. Had it ever been?

He turned the photograph over. On the back, held in place by the laminating film, were pictures of his children; Sarah's was a school snap, taken last year; Sam's was from nursery, shot just a few weeks ago. To the far left of Sam could be seen a painting he had done, pinned to the wall, and he beamed broadly, proud of his artwork, and of the chipped front tooth he was sporting, the result of a recent tumble from a playground slide. His sister, by contrast, looked positively grave, as so often she did, though nonetheless beautiful for that. In subtly different ways, they were equally beautiful, his children, for which their mother was almost solely responsible. They had inherited very few of Colvin's own looks... thankfully, some might say. Staring back at him, now, Sarah's eyes seemed somehow older than her years, forever questioning, doubting; troubled, as if she — like some un-'civilised' native of the bush or jungle — believed the camera was about to steal her soul.

Colvin's fingers traced the outline of his children's golden-brown faces. He loved them. That would always be enough.

The next station, he noticed, was Victoria, and he returned the photographs to his pocket, collected his briefcase from the overhead rack and began to concentrate on his forthcoming appointments. The day was to begin in the office, followed by two visits to clients.

They were not actually clients, as such, but he had always tended to call them that. They were the people whose tax affairs he was paid to investigate, those whose alleged irregularities warranted personal attention from an appointed inspector such as himself.

He had been at the Queen's Club Square offices for ten months now, having made a sideways change of position after the thing (*thing?*) with 'that woman'. Euphemism upon euphemism. As his train pulled in to Victoria, he decided to walk the not inconsiderable distance to the office. After all, he had no meetings first thing, and it was that nice a day.

As it transpired, the day ended far from nicely. Work had been fine, the weather finer still, and his journey home as good as could be expected. His reception though, upon returning home, turned all that had preceded it upside-down. Some past misdemeanour or other, on his part — he never did grasp the essentials — had reared up again in Elspeth's mind and he was presented as he walked through the door with a tirade of abuse. There was no actual shouting, of course. There was no swearing. She was always subtler than that. Within the hour, he felt thoroughly miserable, as if his good day — his bright, Spring-green day — had never happened.

The evening dragged interminably on, and in virtual silence once the children had been put to bed. He had spent longer than usual reading to them upstairs, an extra chapter each — *Winnie-the-Pooh* for Sam,

Alice In Wonderland for Sarah; two of his favourites — in order to delay exposure to Elspeth's steely glares across the living room. He knew he should say something, ask her to explain the reasons for her displeasure, but he lacked the energy, the inclination. Another exercise in conflict avoidance.

Eventually, they went to bed too, still without talking, at a little after ten. Neither slept immediately, but instead lay there, aware of the other's cold proximity, of their conscious efforts not to make any physical contact, however briefly, however innocently. There were times, on the rare occasions when he was awake whilst Elspeth slept, that he would reach out and touch her; not necessarily sexually, but simply to pretend that things were normal again (somehow remaining able to dismiss the very abnormality of such actions). Once more, he tried to stay awake until after she had drifted off, but as usual failed in this and began to slip into another lonely slumber.

The night, however, was far from over.

They had not made love for nearly four months, and so when he felt a light touch, Elspeth's touch, impinge upon his sleep, he wondered at first what it could be. Then, as his dreams faded, and reality supplanted them, he turned to face her. He thought he saw the trace of a smile, visible in the full moon's half-light through the curtains, play across her face. Nervously, he smiled back — still uncertain, still barely conscious — as wordlessly she lifted the duvet and began to guide his hands across her body.

In time, he lifted himself up and over, until he held himself above her, and kissed her full on the lips. Hesitantly at first, she returned the kiss; then forcefully, and with a passion he had thought gone forever. Her eyes, he noticed, were no more awake than his, and he wondered if he dreamed; if they both dreamed.

Again, she lifted the cover slightly, and he reacted at once to this unspoken invitation to slide down under it, gently kissing her immaculate skin as he descended. She did not resist. She responded, fully.

When, a while later, he caressed and kissed his way back along the length of her body and entered her, his sensation of joy was complete...

… but short-lived as he ejaculated inside her almost instantly. There was nothing he could have done to stop it, and her look changed in a second from one of pleasure to one of disgust.

She seemed to sneer; to snarl, almost. Then she shrugged him off and left the bed, going to the bathroom where she stayed for some time.

When, silently, she returned to lie down again, her back towards him, he raised himself on one arm and reached out to touch her shoulder but she flinched. Slowly, he returned his head to the pillow, and stared at the moonwashed ceiling, his eyes wide and pained.

He heard her tears come, then, as he had heard them before; helplessly listening until, eventually, an hour and a lifetime later, sleep returned for them both.

Unsatisfactory as it was, this was the last time they were ever to make love together.

Chapter Six (The Plane Truth)

WHEN SIMON COLVIN next awoke, later that same night, it was still dark.

Something was wrong, though.

It took him a while to realise that he was no longer in bed; that he was standing upright. It was not simply dark, either — not even a moonless dark — it was black. He was cold, shivering.

On a featureless horizon, a crack of light began to show, which soon blossomed and swelled to fill and illuminate the place where he now found himself. It was not sunlight, yet neither did it seem artificial.

He stood, naked, on some kind of immeasurable plain, which was utterly devoid of anything but Simon Colvin. The light did not even cast a shadow to share this barren world with him, if world it was. What he stood on did not appear to be rock, nor any other substance he recognised. It was an unbroken, blemish-free, uniformly pale grey — as, now, was the sky.

Was it even sky? The fact that it was above him was its only semblance to any earthly firmament. A join between 'sky' and 'land', if there was one, was imperceptible until he began to notice flickering patches of darker grey passing overhead, from one horizon to the other, wholly unlike clouds and moving quickly despite the absence around him of the slightest breeze.

He watched these patches, which seemed somehow to move with a purpose (and, he saw now, in opposing directions), for a long time before, with a stiffening neck, he returned his gaze to straight ahead of him…

… and into the eyes of a young woman. She, too, was naked, and very, very beautiful. Her long black hair fell around her shoulders. Unashamedly, she smiled at him, seemingly unaware of or unconcerned with their lack of clothing. "Simon Colvin," she said. It was not a question.

Only then did he begin to wonder where he was, and why. If this woman had not known him, as he certainly did not know her, he might never have questioned his whereabouts; might have been content to assume he merely dreamed a particularly vivid dream. Her confirmation of his name somehow belied this though, and he felt the first tendrils of trepidation creep into his still-drowsy mind which, until then, had all too readily accepted everything it had encountered since waking.

She stood about ten feet from him. His eyes could not help but roam across her perfect body, taking in every curve, before he asked, blushing slightly (though less than he would have expected), "Who are you?"

He realised that his admiration of her had not aroused him; that it was an almost clinical appreciation, as of a statue, and he saw that she seemed to stand in a wholly sexless, unprovocative manner.

He repeated his question, and in no time at all — quite literally — she had halved the distance between them, although he would have sworn she never physically moved.

"Who am I?" A chuckle escaped her lips. It was not a pleasant sound. "I have many names." As an afterthought, she added in a whisper, *"For we are Legion,"* as if to herself, and smiled again.

An horrific revelation began to dawn on him. "It… it's you," he gasped, with considerable effort. She raised a quizzical eyebrow — over, he saw, a purple-tinged eye — as he spoke again. "The one I have to fight."

"That I am," she said. "If fight we must."

"What do you mean?" He knew fear now, like no other he had ever experienced. It gripped at his vitals, and squeezed out of him the ability to think; to ask all but the simplest questions.

"I mean that you cannot possibly win. There is no point in your fighting me. Fight, and you will die; and, I promise you, your death will not be a pleasant one. Refuse to fight, let the inevitable run its course, let the Devil have what is owed him, and you will live, as will those you love."

Sudden fear for his children's safety, previously unimagined — for Elspeth's, too — drove his own from him; was the only thing that could have done so, and he rallied, spitting out: "Touch my family, bitch, and I'll kill you!", venom on every syllable.

If she was taken aback at all, it was for the briefest of moments, before she laughed full in his face. "Fool! Resist me, and you will *all* beg for death." Her own face, all sudden rage, as suddenly calmed, and she was placatory. "I do not wish to harm you. I do not wish to harm anyone. I... I never have. But come against me, Simon Colvin, and harm you I must. I say again, you cannot win. So why fight me?"

"Because *I* must," he said, a strength, a certainty, a conviction, all unrealised, building within him as every second passed. "Because of what will come about if I don't."

"What could *you* know of what is to come? You know nothing. You have not the slightest notion of what you fight, nor of what you fight *for*."

"That's as may be, but I know *who* you fight for, and *what* you stand for, and..."

"... and still you resist me? If so, then you really do have no concept of what you are up against, despite such new-found bravado."

"Hell on Earth, I was told." His confidence continued to grow. "Hell on Earth is what's to come if you win; if I lose. Now, I may have no real idea of what that means — Hell on Earth — but I know that I'll not want to be around to see it. I'd rather die. I'd rather my whole family died."

"Oh, never fear, Simon Colvin. You will. They will. Slowly, and painfully. You haven't the heart for a real fight. You haven't the knowledge..." She stopped, seeming to have been distracted for a moment. "You haven't the heart..." was repeated, and then her eyes closed, and she seemed to be gathering strength, as if to strike out. He steeled himself to receive a blow, took a deep breath and readied himself to fight this woman, here and now.

Her arm did reach out, but not to hit him. It raised slowly, passively, and stopped a few inches from his chest. Her fingers, outspread, closed into a tight ball. Instantly, he felt a pain deep inside him, and clutched at his left breast. "See," she hissed. "See how easily I can snuff you out, little man. You may indeed have the heart to fight me, but I can take that puny organ of yours, and crush it like a dead leaf. You are no match for me."

He screamed, a high-pitched, uncontrolled, thoroughly panicked scream. It ripped from him, with the last of his held breath, and he doubled over and fell to his knees. His chest burned with a fire that threatened to consume his every sense. His eyes saw red through screwed-up lids, and pulsed with his heart's last feeble efforts to circulate life through his body. The red turned to black, and he began to slip away. He had no last thoughts. He was incapable of anything but death.

"WOMAN!"

Though incredibly loud, the voice, a man's, seemed to have come from far away, as if at the end of a long tunnel.

"STOP!"

The pain in Colvin's chest eased a little, but he was still in absolute agony.

"STOP!"

The compression around his heart ceased, and with it a little more of the pain; he fell full-length onto the ground, drawing one excruciating breath that tore at his throat and seared his lungs. He tried, and failed, to open his eyes.

"WOMAN. YOU ARE NOT WELCOME HERE. BEGONE!"

Colvin heard her yell: "I will not…"

"YOU HAVE NO CHOICE. I COMMAND IT!"

"Damn you, I'll…"

"YOU CANNOT DAMN ME, WOMAN. YOU HAVE NO POWER OVER SUCH AS I."

Slowly, painfully, Colvin rolled over onto his back and forced his eyes to open. Extending high into the 'sky', thousands of feet tall, there was Dylan, the angel — a gigantic Dylan — naked, also — more beautiful than ever, radiating strength and (*what's the word?*) goodness — staring calmly down at the two figures so far below him.

"BEGONE!"

"No. I'll…" shouted the woman, but her words faded, as did she, into particles of dust that swirled in a miniature tornado and then disappeared, with a last sound like a tired, desperate sigh.

The giant figure above Colvin turned its attention to him, and a hand, hundreds of feet across, reached down towards him. It was the last thing he saw as his agony-racked, exhausted brain refused to take anything else in, and shut down into blissful unconsciousness.

When Simon Colvin next awoke, he was sitting upon a small, varnished bench, in what appeared to be a park, in front of a brook which bubbled along its course across small rocks and pebbles with a motion that soothed its way into his still-aching body and calmed him. A light breeze rustled reeds on the brook's banks, and helped a willow cry its pale green tears into the water. Daffodils, tulips, bluebells and snowdrops tipped their hats in his direction from a raised bed to his left. The sky — a real sky — was blue and cloudless, and the sun shone brightly and warmly. The grass under his bare feet was slightly damp, and had a fresh, heady, new-mown scent to it. He breathed in, deeply, and was reminded of his recent ordeal by a scorching pain across his chest. He coughed, involuntarily, and the pain increased.

"How do you feel?" It was Dylan asking, sitting next to him, on his right.

"Terrific, thanks," he wheezed, and rubbed at his chest, grimacing, noticing for the first time that he was dressed now, in a loose-fitting, rather drab robe, a little like a dressing gown. "Next silly question…"

Dylan reached a hand inside Colvin's robe, and placed the palm flat against his left breast. Immediately the discomfort lessened until it was barely noticeable, and was replaced with a warmth and a feeling of wellbeing.

Not certain that he could cope with the answer, but because he had to, Colvin asked, "What happened?"

The angel sat back. "You met your adversary."

It was not exactly an explanation, but it would do for now. "Where were we?"

"Limbo."

He needed more. "Dylan, I know she was my... my adversary. I thought she was supposed to be hundreds of years old. Why wasn't she, and what do you mean by Limbo?"

"If I may, I'll answer the second part to begin with."

"Okay." For the first time, Colvin realised that Dylan had wholly dropped his hippy persona, and also that he no longer bore a pair of golden wings. Instead he was dressed in simple, blue denim jeans, and a cotton T-shirt, resembling an American football player's top and bearing the legend 'Conductor 71', an in-joke which was totally lost on Colvin. On his feet were once-white, rather scuffed sneakers.

"Limbo is exactly what you might expect it to be," said Dylan, "a plane of existence which is not on Earth, nor in Heaven, nor Hell, but somehow between all three."

"Of course," said Colvin, as if understanding every word, whilst making it perfectly clear that he had not.

"It's harder to explain in any other way. Suffice to say that it was the only place where the two of you could have met, at least in the states in which you did."

"And they were...?"

"Well, for you, in a dream state. Even now, as you and I talk here, you are actually at home, in bed, asleep."

"And for her...?"

"She would have to have been in a trancelike state, in order to enter Limbo, and in order to draw you here. It is why you were both naked. Nothing material can enter Limbo."

"Then where are we now?"

"In a pleasanter aspect of that same plane. What you see around you, what we are wearing and so on, is all illusion, but it is an allowed illusion, for a short time at least."

"So, she wasn't old because she wasn't real, right?"

"Correct. She could have appeared to you in any form at all, human or otherwise. I think we can assume that what we saw was she, as she might have looked a hundred and fifty years ago."

"Beautiful."

"And deadly."

"Dylan, could she really have killed me, there — here, I mean — if we're not really here at all?"

"Oh, yes, all too easily. Her power is that great."

A thought occurred to Colvin. "What is her name?"

"She told you. She has many; has had a great many, over the years. Give her any name and she grows in power. Refuse her a name and her power weakens. I call her Woman. For that is what she is."

"Not all women?" Colvin struggled to keep pace with so much new information. "Not as in Womankind?" It seemed a strange question, even as he asked it.

"No. Womankind is a great force for good in the world. Perhaps the greatest. No, she is but a single, very powerful woman. She is your adversary."

"Hold on a moment. You knew what she said to me. How long were you watching?"

"The whole time. She believed you were both unobserved. Such things rarely go unobserved. She…"

"She could've killed me! Would've killed me, if…"

"… if I hadn't stopped it. Yes. But I did stop it. That is all that matters."

"So why did you wait so long?"

"We had to see how you… performed."

"And?"

"You did very well, Simon."

"When she could attack me, kill me, so easily, you reckon I did *well*? How can I fight against that?"

"Perhaps you can't, but at least you now know what you are up against."

Colvin resisted giving voice to a comment that had sprung to mind. Instead he looked around him, and then chuckled.

"What's so funny?" asked Dylan.

"Well, we shouldn't be here."

The angel looked puzzled.

"We should be in a drawing room. All good mysteries end up in a drawing room, with everything being explained to characters and reader alike, and I can't help this urge I've got to utter the immortal phrase, 'What I don't understand is this…'."

That joke, too, was lost on its recipient. One all.

"The only thing is," he continued, "that I've got a hundred and one questions that need answering."

"So try me."

"Okay. Let's start with… why me? Why here? Why now?"

"Why you? I thought we had already explained that that's not really known. We only know it has to be you. As to why here… in Limbo, you mean?"

"No. Far from it? I mean why England? Why London, assuming that's where the fight will be? Look at all the cities there are in the world. All the countries, most larger, some holier (allegedly) than England. Why there? Why not Israel, in Megiddo —" at which the angel revealed impressed astonishment — "the source of the word Armageddon." Colvin grinned. "You're not the only ones who've been doing research, you know."

Smiling back, Dylan said, "The venue was not ours for the choosing, either. The woman was picked, as you know, many years ago, although she has not long since been told of her destiny in this respect. Perhaps part of your suitability for the rôle is no more than proximity."

"Okay, so next: why now? Why Armageddon, now?"

"Well, from what I gather, the rules state…"

Colvin snorted, derisively.

"What's wrong?" asked Dylan.

"I've always found it kind of hard to understand the concept of *rules*, in *war*, let alone in Armageddon. It's ridiculous!"

"Nevertheless, rules there are, and rules we must abide by. Those rules — *conditions*, if you prefer — state that Armageddon can be called for at any time, and by either party. Until now, neither has seen fit to do so; has had no reason to. Then, from what we can gather, relatively recently, the Devil sought some kind of reconciliation with his Maker, and was flatly refused. This, as you can imagine, did not please him. I understand a degree of abasement was involved which, when it proved fruitless, caused certain irrevocable oaths to be uttered, and before we knew what had happened, well… there it was… Armageddon."

"Just like that?"

"Just like that."

"And do we know when it begins?"

"Simon, I believe it already has. I think you have just been granted an opening salvo. I expect the woman needed to size you up; to persuade you, if she could, not to resist her; to kill you if you refused. In that, at least, she failed."

"Another question…"

"Yes?"

"Why, when you appeared, were you so huge?"

"There is no such thing as scale in Limbo. If you but knew it, it was not I that was huge, but the two of you who were tiny. I suspect it was all she had the strength to control."

Yet another thought, one of so many, now occurred to Colvin. "When I first arrived there — here — there were shapes in the sky, dark patches crossing it. What were they?"

"Shades," answered Dylan. The word rang a bell with Colvin, but he could not make the connection. The angel continued: "I understand that when you… toured Heaven, you commented on the shades of Hell that you noticed in some of the booths. You were told, I believe, that such shades, both of Heaven and of Hell, appear to cross between the two planes and somehow interact with the residents of each. It is through Limbo that these shades must pass, on their journeys to and fro. That is what you saw here."

"What are they, exactly?"

"No-one really knows. What we do know is that those coming to Heaven, from Hell, are inherently wicked — evil, even — and that they can be waylaid along their paths by one such as your adversary. They can be made to do the bidding of anyone strong enough to summon and control them."

"Demons?"

"If you like. The woman's last victim, an innocent man she did not even know, was killed by just such a 'demon'. It never even had to touch him. He died of fright. You should be wary, if ever such a creature is sent against you."

"*Wary*? Something of an understatement. How about scared shitless?"

"If you like," said Dylan again, distracted this time, as he began to glance around them. When Colvin did the same, he noticed that their surroundings — the park, the brook, the flora — were beginning to shimmer, becoming unstable.

"What's happening?"

"Time's up," said Dylan. "Limbo cannot sustain even an illusion of the material world for very long. We are being ejected."

"But…"

"Hush! I have one more thing I must tell you, that has been discovered. It is important. You must seek a weapon. It is a powerful weapon. It will help you in your battle."

"What kind of a weapon?"

"We do not know. We are trying to find out. The woman will be seeking it, also. You must find it before she does. It will help you, possibly, to win."

"And if she gets to it first?"

"Then she cannot lose."

It was the last thing Colvin heard, before all turned suddenly to black.

When Simon Colvin next awoke, it was to the sound of his alarm clock. To his left, Elspeth stirred, woke, and then arose. Their eyes met, for a second or two, as she crossed to the bathroom. Neither of them spoke of the night's bitter disappointment.

Neither of them spoke.

Reminiscence (3)

S HE SITS, AND she waits. In her lap is a small black clutch-bag. Her hands grip it tightly.

She opens her eyes briefly, shuts them again, and remembers.

She had remembered killing Richard, her husband. Now she remembers failing to kill Simon Colvin.

She remembered being ejected from Limbo by that interfering angel, just as she had Colvin at her mercy.

She had been torn, violently, back into the material world, back into her corporeal body, which lay in the centre of a room set aside for her Summonings. A pain, which she could only assume was akin to that of childbirth, poured through her, outward from her navel, as her spirit form reoccupied her flesh and her bones. She yelled out, and dragged in deep breaths that seemed to take an age to fill her lungs.

Slowly, tentatively, she sat up, and eventually gathered strength enough to stand, shaking with the effort, before steadying herself and walking to the full-length mirror on a wall opposite the closed-curtained windows.

Wistfully, she looked at the reflection of her withered, wrinkled, ancient body, and remembered all too clearly what it had felt like so recently to occupy a form over which the skin was tight and smooth, blemish-free and beautiful. She looked at her hair, frosty white where once was a lustrous, raven black — lank and lifeless now — and she sighed.

She had no time for this. Introspection was a luxury she denied herself, despite its prevalence among the more long-lived of the damned.

She turned away from the mirror, and began to dress. Her body still ached, but the pain of her recent exertions was already fading.

She had learned one important thing. Simon Colvin was not a supernatural foe. Nor, it seemed, did he have any real knowledge of, or access to, powers such as hers. She knew that the angels could not become directly involved in their battle, not on Earth, and she was bolstered by thoughts of almost certain success.

She could take her time over this; indulge herself, enjoy the fight, savour the victory. She had all she needed to take down this man, this Colvin, whom she had now failed once to kill. He did indeed have heart (not to mention a powerful ally or two), but she would soon make him regret his ignorant refusals. She would not fail again.

Then she remembered she did not yet have all she needed. There was one more item. The demon had said so…

… and much more.

She had been asleep, several nights before, when it had come to her. She needed a great deal of sleep, these days, to keep her strength up, but she always slept lightly, and knew in an instant when she was no longer alone in the bedroom.

She had opened her eyes, and saw in a corner, in the half-light, a creature of singular repugnance. She had seen too much horror in her long life — caused too much — to be overly perturbed.

"What do you want?" she asked, simply.

"A message from our Master," came the wetly whispered reply. Lips, if there were any, had not moved. The voice was inside her head. "A task. A death."

"But payment has been made for this year."

"Another. A last. Do this, and you are released."

She sucked in a sharp, surprised breath, refusing to believe what she had just heard. "Released?" she croaked.

"Released from your bond. Free. Free to live. Free to die. Whichever.

This I have been told to impart. Succeed, and you are released. Fail, and your life on Earth is over. You will be delivered unto Hell."

Her old, tired heart pounded in her chest at these words, and all that they implied. Could she really be free; become free? She was wary. "Who must I kill? Why?"

So the demon had explained, in its own stilted, somewhat archaic way, what was expected of her. Finally, it revealed the need she had to find a certain artefact, to aid her in the forthcoming battle.

"You have to seek something. With it, you will win. Without it, you must still win, but your task will be harder."

"What is it that I need to find?"

"A grail," said the demon. "Possibly *the* Grail. We know not."

"But surely one such as I would be denied the presence of the Grail?"

"The one true Grail, if that it proves to be, takes many forms. No creature of Hell could behold its first, its purest form."

She looked at the demon then, that creature of Hell, and took unvoiced exception to being likened to it — grouped together with it — as a fellow. Instead, she merely said, "Where do I find it, this grail?"

"We know not. When the time is right, it will beckon you, and your enemy also. You must locate it first. It will be your greatest weapon…"

… and, with that, the demon had disappeared, leaving nothing of its presence there but a slightly stale, unpleasant odour.

It was not the first visitation of this sort that she had received, and she had become used to most demons' somewhat rapid departures. She had the feeling that existence on Earth, however fleeting, was painful for them; that once their allotted task was completed, they were anxious to return to whence they came.

So many years. Many such visitations, though never of such import. In all that time, she had not once seen Him.

She thought back now, to their first, their only meeting; how He had seduced her with His talk of an Age of Women, with His promises of power, and of money, and of eternal life. She had been so young, then; so naïve, so foolish, so willing to believe. Now, she had lived for so very long, and had yet to see anything like an Age of Women come about. Oh, there had been improvements, no doubt, but token ones. Gestures.

It was still, and always would be, an Age of Men. As for power, and money, and life itself — however eternal — she had come to loathe each one. For a while, they had served their purpose. She had used them all, to the full. She had travelled much, seen much, done much; achieved little.

The Devil had seduced her with such ease; mentally, at first, and then physically.

She was His, had always been His, thought she always would be His. Now she had the chance to rid herself of Him, of her curse, her damnation, and to win her freedom. A natural death was all she wished for.

She must not fail.

From that moment on, she had begun to plan. She tracked down her new foe, Simon Colvin, and had even followed him home from work one evening — caught the same train, found out where he lived — and now their first encounter had taken place. It had not been the quick and easy victory she had hoped for, but it had shown her much, and now she must plot her next move.

The battle for everything was about to begin.

⛤ ⛤ ⛤

All this she remembers.

Still she sits. Still she waits…

Chapter Seven (Another Tuesday)

Simon Colvin sat upon a bench, on his home train station's London-bound platform, awaiting the arrival of the 08:08 to Victoria. He was late for work.

It had been an odd kind of morning, so far. *Odd*, he thought as he sat, staring ahead but seeing nothing, *is a very good word for it. And rather an odd night, too.*

He was numb. He had arisen shortly after Elspeth, performed his ablutions, helped to get Sarah ready for school, Sam for nursery, in a silence to which they were all now accustomed. The adults spoke only in response to their children. All else around the house — breakfast and the like — was conducted as an elaborate mime, his Pierrot to her Columbine. Even his tardiness passed without comment, and Elspeth eventually left with the children, unnecessarily early, before he had set off for the station. There he now sat — numb — in a kind of dazed semi-reality through which he continued to function, outwardly normal, as if an automaton.

Though he had perfect memories of every single thing that had befallen him over the previous eleven hours, his mind refused to let him concentrate on any more than a fraction of them at one time, and so they had a disjointed, episodic feel to them, and kept changing, in his mind, the order in which they had occurred, so that all became a blurred, fragmented montage.

It was likely this mental filtering of his thoughts saved Colvin's sanity; saved him from running screaming over into the chasm of madness that seemed to gape open in front of him, always just beyond reach, kept at bay by a mind that protected him out of nothing but its own instinctive self-preservation. It knew that, for the moment at least, he was unable to cope with any more than he absolutely had to in order to get through a normal working day.

So, when his train arrived, Colvin arose, walked forward, opened the door and sat down in the carriage, barely aware that he had done any of these things.

In a little under an hour and a half, he was at the door of his offices. The first time he spoke to another adult that day was to greet a colleague who was on his way out as Colvin came in. The colleague made some reference to his hour of arrival — twice late, this week — but the remark went unanswered.

He made himself a mug of tea, and sat at his desk, staring hard at his diary until the words scribbled there, at first a mere blur, began to come into focus. He had an appointment at midday, with a new client, a Mrs. Catherine Beauchamp, of Dan Leno Walk, SW6. It took him some time to find the street — tiny, no more than a mews — in his *Geographers' A-Z London Atlas*, squeezed in between the Fulham and King's Roads; then he reached further across his desk for the woman's file, one amongst many.

C. Beauchamp, Mrs.; thirty-five years old; authoress (*a crime writer*, someone had handwritten in the margin, apparently for his information. He had not heard of her. Perhaps she used a nom de plume); details of irregularities: well, it seemed that her own tax office claimed she owed a healthy six-figure sum to the Revenue, which she denied, blaming an incompetent ex-accountant for any discrepancies — *no excuse* — and it appeared that the usual seven-year period for tax records' investigation had been increased by his Special Commissioners. He had ten years' worth of this woman's affairs to plough through; a long job.

He read on, reaching for his mug, only to discover he had finished his tea with no recollection of having done so. As he stood to go to the kitchen and make another, he glanced casually at a calendar on the wall, issued by the British Heart Foundation, and before he knew it he was clutching at his chest as a stabbing pain — a mere echo of the previous night's — assailed him. The mug slipped from his fingers and fell to the floor where it bounced on the carpet tiles and disappeared under his desk. He sank to his knees, closed his eyes, but could still see the calendar's logo of a heart, which seemed to pulse with the rhythm of his own, loud in his ears, threatening to burst as it was crushed beneath sorcerous fingers. He had great difficulty breathing, and yanked at his collar in an attempt to loosen it and his tie in one go. He needed air; fresh air, but was too weak to rise. Instead he tried to calm his ragged breaths and racing pulse from where he was kneeling, beside his desk, as if in prayer.

He had no idea how long he remained like that, but it could not have been as long as it seemed, for no-one found him there or even passed his office's door. Slowly, his composure returned, and he felt he could stand without fainting or vomiting. Using the desk as a prop, he dragged himself upright, and paused whilst a wave of nausea swept through him.

It passed, and was replaced by a desperate need to get out, into the open. Grabbing his briefcase, he stuffed the Beauchamp woman's file roughly into it, and half-walked, half-ran for the exit, where another sunny Spring morning's weather washed over him as he drew its air into his lungs.

Realising he would be far too early for his appointment, if he were to go straight there now, he turned instead away from that direction and headed north, towards the traffic-clogged Talgarth Road and beyond, aiming for Olympia where he stopped, only partially aware of how he had got there.

Concentrating on the task at hand — getting to his appointment at the correct time — he then took a slow, meandering route back southwards, through Earl's Court's side-streets, lined with blossom-laden magnolia and mock cherry, a copper beech, even the vibrant electric blue of an early-blooming Californian lilac (*ceanothus*, he told himself absently; the only Latin name he could ever recall for anything).

The trees' scents, almost overpowering at times, had a healing effect on his mind, so that by the time he arrived at Dan Leno Walk he felt more than capable of dealing with his business, and that of his client, quite adequately.

A large, ornate and somewhat incongruous bell-pull confronted him as he arrived at the small townhouse's simple Carolinian front door. He tugged at it, but could hear no sound from within and so decided also to tap at the far less ostentatious chrome knocker.

In time, the door opened, and there stood a slightly built, redheaded woman in a full-length, patterned cotton dressing gown. She did not seem surprised to see him; did not seem caught unawares, and this was confirmed by her greeting: "Mr. Colvin."

He nodded. "Mrs. Beauchamp." He pronounced her name in the French: 'Bo-shom', and she corrected him with the English: 'Beecham'.

"Like the powders?" he said, smiling.

"Like the Place." She returned his smile warmly, and invited him in. "And it's 'Ms.', not 'Mrs.'," she called out as she led him up the steep, print-lined stairway. "Never has been. I don't know where they got that from. Do you think that could be part of my tax problems, if the Revenue thinks I'm married?"

"I don't know, Ms... *Beauchamp* —" he emphasised the name's Anglicism — "that's what we're here to find out."

"Coffee?"

He was not supposed to accept refreshments, but often did. "Tea, please, if you have it," he said, without hesitation.

He was astonished at the ease with which he had slipped into a wholly familiar work mode, when not long since he had been reduced to a quivering wreck by a wall calendar's logo, and only hours before had been genuinely struggling for his life on some alien plane of existence.

Even his mind seemed more prepared, now, to allow him this reminder of recent events, less fearful of its repercussions, as he was led into a small galley kitchen at the top of the stairs.

"Ms. Beauchamp," he began, but she interrupted him with another friendly smile.

"Cathy, please."

"Cathy. Do you know what we are here to achieve? What I have to go through with you..."

... and so it began, and so it continued, over several more cups of herbal tea — not really to his taste — as they went through the preliminaries of a long and complicated tax investigation, of which he had done so many.

Cathy Beauchamp proved remarkably forthcoming, candidly providing him with all the information she could readily lay her hands on. She apologised for being a little foggy-headed on specifics, the results of both a brain for which figures meant little, and the onset of a cold (hence the dressing gown; she had laid in, hoping to sleep it off). Colvin said that he could not remember ever having been greeted by a client in such attire. She replied that he should count himself lucky she had remembered their appointment, otherwise she might have come to the door naked. He blushed.

At a little after five in the afternoon she suggested, in lieu of tea, a glass of white wine and, before he had considered his customary principle never to imbibe whilst 'on duty', he readily agreed. She poured them a large glass each, of a well chilled Sancerre, and proposed a move from her rather cramped office into the living room, taking their papers with them.

Several glasses later, as the sun began to set through trees visible from the sliding doors leading to a small roof terrace — their papers long ignored on the low table between them — she asked if he was married.

"Yes," he answered, simply, unperturbed by a question which seemed a natural extension of the way their conversation had been heading. It had been some time since they last discussed anything tax-related.

"Happily?"

"No." This question surprised him — as did his answer — then he asked, "Why?"

"It's just that you look so sad, so… haunted."

He wondered what she would have thought if he told her of what was really likely to have given him that haunted look; of the previous night's encounter in Limbo. Instead, he just looked at her, noticing for the first time the way the sun's last embers played across her long hair, which he had thought of at first as near ginger, like his, but which now appeared a deep, fiery auburn.

"I *do* apologise," she said suddenly. "It must seem terribly forward of me, asking such things. The insular life of a writer, you see, makes one forget certain accepted graces. That, and an overly inquisitive nature. Please don't think me rude, or — heaven forbid! — that I'm coming on to you at all. Oh, dear, have I offended you? It's the wine. I shouldn't have… I'm sorry, I'm babbling."

He smiled, amused by her obvious embarrassment. "Not at all. I've enjoyed talking with you, and I promise you I'm not offended. But now I think I should be going. Same time next week?"

"Yes, that's fine," she said. "Do you have children?"

They looked at each other then, in mutual and humorous appreciation of her relentless, not to mention tactless, probing, and they laughed out loud together, long and hard.

Once their mirth had subsided, allowing him to speak, he answered her: "Yes, I do," and before he knew what was happening he was telling her everything about his marriage; of his hopes and fears for its future; of far more than he ever should have done (though he mentioned nothing of the more supernatural goings-on). Something, somewhere, was nagging at him that this was wrong, but he could not help himself. A dam, once cracked, will soon burst apart, and nothing can stop such a torrent from pouring forth.

Cathy Beauchamp did nothing but listen. As a slight distraction, a need to ease the intensity with which he spoke, they had cleared their papers and glasses away, and now stood in the kitchen, as far apart from each other as its limited dimensions would allow.

As suddenly as his confession — there seemed no other word for it — began, so it ceased, to be followed by a not necessarily awkward silence between them.

Neither moved for several minutes; neither made a sound, until Cathy cleared her throat and began to take a step forward. Stopping, hesitating, she said, "So sad. You look so very sad. I'd like, if I may, to give you a hug. That's all. I don't…"

She left the sentence unfinished, as if confused by her own motives, and she moved towards him. He did nothing to stop her, and before he knew it she was in front of him, her arms around his shoulders in an embrace which, admittedly, was about as platonic as such a gesture could be.

His own arms remained at his side, although they had involuntarily twitched, at first, with an instinct to return the hug. He resisted. Her head was close to his chin, and he could smell her hair's perfume. He knew that he had only to lower his own head and his lips would meet her brow.

Above all else, he recalled another time, another 'client', and restrained himself from reacting in any way at all.

Slowly, she drew away from him, and stood very still. "I'm sorry."

"Don't be." His voice shook.

"What… what do you want?"

"From what?"

"From life?" Somehow, even this was not as peculiar a question as it seemed.

"I want my life *back*, Cathy. I want my *wife* back." He fought against an unexpected onrush of tears.

"Do you?"

"Yes."

"Then you had better go home to her," she said. "It's late."

He glanced at his watch, and found it hard to believe that it was after ten. "I guess I'd better."

The evening was cool, as Simon Colvin walked towards Fulham Broadway Underground station, and his head was surprisingly uncluttered. He even whistled slightly, almost chirpily, in rhythm with his steps, feeling strangely elated. For the first time since 'that woman', he had been tempted (or did he only imagine he had?), and had resisted that temptation. This was something to be proud of. Wasn't it?

He did not notice footfalls behind him until someone spoke.

"Mind if I walk with you a while?"

Colvin stopped, turned, and saw Dylan, the angel, standing in the light of a street-lamp. "Sure."

They set off again together, equally jaunty, and chatted at first like two old friends who had just met for the first time in a while. Banter. As they neared the station Dylan said, "Long day?"

Colvin did not seem to grasp his meaning.

"I meant you seem to have had a long day, a long meeting."

"Oh, yes, that's right. A client meeting. Nice lady; very kind."

"Kind?"

"Yes." If he noticed the angel's subtly altered, delving tone at all, he chose to ignore it.

"Tell me," asked Dylan, "what do you want?"

"From what?" An echo.

"From life."

Colvin was suddenly on the defensive, a confused and confusing mixture of defiance, protectiveness and... (*guilt?*) tumbling within him. "Have you been watching me again?"

Dylan was unfazed. "Not all of the time."

"Today? Were you there today, at Cathy's?"

"Cathy?"

"Don't fuck with me, Dylan, you know who I mean! The... the client I've spent all day with. Were you there?"

"No."

"Then what do you mean, what do I want from life?"

"Just what I say. A couple of months ago, you were a normal, run-of-the-mill tax inspector, with a normal, run-of-the-mill tax inspector's worries; you were a husband and father, with all the problems that can entail, and you knew nothing of your fate; of the fate of the world, nor ever imagined you would be playing such a major rôle in it. You have to admit, your life has taken something of a turn in recent weeks. Now, with all you have to do, everything you know, I wondered what you actually want from all this?"

Colvin was quiet for a while. Was this some sort of test? They had reached the station, and stood just within its entranceway as a cold wind was now blowing, and an unseasonally icy rain had begun to fall from what had earlier been a cloudless sky. "I'm sorry, Dylan, I didn't mean to snap at you. It's just that you're the second person to ask me that today, though for entirely different reasons, I think."

"And what was your answer?"

"Then, as now, I want my life back. I want my wife back."

"Do you? Do you really?"

There was a small, barely perceptible hesitation before Colvin answered, "Yes."

"That's all?"

"What do you mean, '*that's all?*'?"

"Exactly that. The fate of the world is in your hands, and you want to save your marriage."

"Is there anything so wrong with that?" The same mixed emotions — defiance, protectiveness, guilt — arose in Colvin again. "I never asked for this... this fate of mine. I never wanted it, any of it! I don't want it now. All I ever seem to have wanted was for things to be the way they were, before..." His voice trailed off.

"Before?"

"Nothing. It doesn't matter." He was sullen now.

"Simon, are you sure that's what you really want?"

Colvin saw no point in answering. If Dylan was watching as often as he suspected, then the angel must *surely* know what was going on between him and Elspeth; must realise how important it was...

He was about to try explaining this when a wave of frustration swept through him, and his mind changed. "I've got a train to catch," was all he said, and he stalked off towards the ticket barrier. He was not followed.

By the time Colvin got home, it was almost midnight. The rain had turned to sleet, but he hardly noticed it.

Every light in the house seemed to be on; every curtain open. A tight knot twisted his stomach as he turned the key in the door's latch and stepped through into the hallway. He left his briefcase there, and walked into the living room to find Elspeth sitting in an armchair. Saying nothing, she stood, walked past him, left the room and went upstairs.

A little later, having gone around shutting curtains and turning off lights, he joined her in the bedroom. She was already in bed, eyes wide, staring at the ceiling. He undressed, got in next to her, and assumed an identical position.

After half an hour, neither of them had moved, nor showed any signs of sleep. Suddenly Elspeth spoke, one ice-chilled sentence: "I think it is time we considered getting a divorce."

Then silence.

It was not the first time he had heard these words, but it was the first time he had not reacted. Normally, his response would be to beg for it not to be so, to plead for forgiveness. This time, he simply continued to stare upwards, and said absolutely nothing. There seemed nothing to say.

It was the longest, coldest night either of them ever spent.

Chapter Eight (Endings And Encounters)

THE FOLLOWING MORNING, Simon Colvin arose first, and pulled the curtains back to reveal a silver and white sea of beauty. Cold as an iceberg. The silver flakes gracefully floated to the creamy white earth. Children in the adjoining gardens shouted joyfully whilst running around white snowmen. Their voices sounded so excited as they ran around the bare trees, topped with white stars so tiny and cold. The beautiful sea of silver had small footprints of their Blue Persian cat. Their warm pond was now an icy transparent floor. The birds in the sky of white flew around, confused, seeking a warm place and wondering whether or not it was time to fly south. The white lane beyond the garden had tracks of cars. Their roofs were a brilliant, dazzling white, with cat footprints on their white bonnets. The joyful children ran to their houses, with silver flakes on the scarlet roofs…

He blinked, once, and this fairy-tale vision faded, at least partially. There were no children, no snowmen, but there was snow, lots of snow. The trees were not bare; their Spring foliage was laden with powder and their boughs sagged, threatening to snap under the additional weight. Birds in the grey, threatening sky really did seem to be as puzzled by the scene as he was. This was supposed to be Spring, not Winter.

He turned away from the window, shrugging, and began to dress. Elspeth got up and did likewise, noticing but also not commenting on the peculiar scene outside.

At breakfast, while their children played upstairs, the radio told them that most trains had been cancelled due to the bad weather. Unexpectedly, Elspeth responded to this, and asked if Simon would be going into work. She seemed almost hopeful that he would not.

"I think I'll take the car," he said. "It'll be a little slick, but most people won't be bothering at all, and the new snow should be safe enough to drive on."

"Don't go."

He stared at her.

"Simon, please don't go."

"I have to. I've got meetings."

"Stay. I want... need... to talk."

"What about?"

"About us. I think it's time... time we started to... mend; to make things better between us. It's been going on for too long. I want us to be... together again."

There. It was said. He sat, stunned; too stunned to speak, as he took in what this meant, and what it meant to him. He had heard the words which, for the last year, he had longed to hear. He realised he should be ecstatic; swinging from lampshades, shouting from rooftops. She wanted him back. She actually wanted him back. Instead, he felt nothing but a strange, hollow emptiness, colder even than the scene outside. What he thought he had wished for, for so long, had finally come about, and he was no longer sure that he wanted it at all. This was crazy! Of course he wanted it! But no, he knew, deep inside, that he did not. He had clung for so many months, to the need for an ideal, that he had not even noticed the erosion over that time of whatever mortar had originally bound them together, made them a couple — husband and wife — the erosion of that very ideal. He was drained, he realised; had been drained of everything he believed he held most dear.

He looked at Elspeth. Whatever that look showed, he saw her reaction to it as tears brimmed around her eyes.

"*Oh, Simon, please don't go!*" she breathed.

"I told you, I have meetings."

"No! Please don't leave me!"

Until that moment, he had not even realised that he might. Now, instead of reacting to her pleas, he found himself trying to explain to Elspeth the way he felt; the *lack* of feeling he was experiencing, but she seemed incapable of comprehension.

Eventually, her demeanour changed from one of conciliatory supplication to one of affronted outrage, and she gave vent to a fury he had not seen since the day after he had told her, so many months before, of 'that woman'. Any last vestiges of feeling that might have remained were driven from him under this onslaught, and he began, automatically, to prepare for work, as if he could not hear anything she said. Only her last words, before she sank into a breathless, raging silence, got through to him: "Well, if you're going to go, damn you, go now!"

He turned to face her. "Now?"

"Now!"

"What do we tell the children?"

"*I'm* not going to tell them anything. *You're* going to tell them you're leaving them! Sarah! Sam! Come here, please." She somehow managed to make this last summoning almost lightweight, holding none of the vitriol which had preceded it.

They heard footfalls on the stairs, as their children descended, into the mælstrom. Sam, their youngest, entered the living room first, looked at his parents and simply burst into tears, running to bury his face in the cushions of the sofa. He could have had no idea what was about to happen, but the atmosphere was molasses-thick with anger and pain and sorrow. Sarah came into the room, and gave them all an enquiring glance which belied her tender age.

Simon could barely speak. "Kids," he croaked, "come here, please. I've got something to tell you both." Sam refused to move, and so Simon went to the sofa and sat down, beckoning Sarah over to join him. Tears were now streaming down her face, too, but she made no sound, and her teeth bit down hard on her bottom lip in an attempt not to surrender to whatever she was feeling.

So, cuddling them both, he told them that he was leaving; that he would no longer be living with them any more. Sam continued to bawl, his head now buried in his father's chest. Sarah still said nothing, but drew blood from her lip as she failed to fight back the weeping from eyes that silently implored Simon to stay; that begged to understand what was happening to them all.

There was no explanation; none *he* could clearly comprehend, let alone they, and so eventually he stood, and his place was taken by Elspeth, who cradled their children in a rocking motion, all three of them moving to and fro; all three of them openly sobbing. Only Elspeth spoke as, through her tears, she pleaded with him once more to remain.

Instead, he grabbed his briefcase from the hallway floor, opened the front door to the bitter, snowy world outside, and turned to face his family through the living-room doorway. Now his own tears finally came, and the last image he had of them all was one blurred into a single, rocking, weeping mass of agonised heartache, as he turned again, out into the freezing air, and closed the door behind him.

His face seemed to rime in an instant with an icy frost as his tears chilled upon it. He stumbled down the drive towards the car, got in, started the engine and pulled away, the rear end slipping in the new-fallen snow until its tyres found ruts in the road which they could follow like a train on rails. Without this assistance to his motion, it is likely he would have travelled no farther than the first parked car, into which he would have careered, his vision still denied him by his grief.

Once around the first corner — somehow — he half-pulled, half-slid into the kerbside and stopped the car, before letting rip with a cry of such terrible anguish that it seemed to fill the whole world. Spasms racked his body as he poured out all of his emotions, some still half-formed and as yet unrealised, in one long, seemingly endless torrent.

It was over.

The roads were all but deserted. No-one appeared to be driving. No-one appeared to be walking. It was as if he were the only person left alive, as Colvin drove through a London transformed. The capital bore a shroud of virgin whiteness that deadened all sound, all colour. It suited his mood, and he could not help but appreciate its fittingness to the day's events. He could still hardly believe what had happened. Was it really all over? Was he really never going back through that door? He held at bay any logic which told him that of course he would do, if only to collect his belongings. That did not fit in with his current desire for melodramatic reflection.

So absorbed was he, in this somehow cathartic meditation, that he did not at first hear the voice. "*Colvin*," it murmured, at a volume so low that it matched and was almost lost in the gusts of wind that still blew flurries of snow across the road.

He did not hear it the second time it called, nor the third, but upon its fourth utterance he turned his head from side to side, believing he must have imagined that someone whispered his name.

"*Colvin!*" This time it was not quiet. It was loud, in his ear, so close that he could almost have sworn he felt its speaker's breath on his neck.

"Who's there?" he cried out, knowing how ridiculous that was when he was obviously alone in the car.

"*How do you like my little snowstorm, Colvin?*"

It was her, he knew. The woman. His adversary. "Where are you?"

"*Everywhere. Nowhere. Anywhere. You will never know, until it is too late. I have seen into your home, little man. They are still crying, you know. They miss you. They need you. Why aren't you there with them?*"

"Shut up!" he yelled. He could not listen to this.

"*Will you not be there to help them? No. I do not think you will, for I have other plans for you, after which you will be of no use to anyone, let alone to those who still love you.*"

"Shut up! Shut up! Shut up!" He was screaming now, shaking his head from side to side, unwary of the car's erratic motion, its increasing speed.

"*Who is that?*" snapped the voice, as if in surprised recognition. He jerked his head up in reaction to this and glared out of the windscreen in front of him. As a mist of windswept snow cleared before him, he saw Elspeth, Sarah and Sam standing in the middle of the road, ghostly pale. He stamped on the car's brake pedal and felt the vehicle slide inexorably towards his family…

… and straight through them, as they burst apart in an explosion of snow. In front of him now was a high wall, previously unseen, as he skidded out of control across a T-junction and mounted the kerb, heading for destruction. The car's bonnet struck the wall and he was tossed forward, his seat belt scorching his neck. The kerb, though, had robbed the car of much of its speed, and what should have been a fatal crash had merely dented — albeit badly — the front of the vehicle.

He threw the gearbox into reverse, and backed away from the wall, leaving débris on the pavement, into the road again. There, in front of him now, was the woman who had caused all of this. He knew it was her. Snowy illusion or not, he was determined to mow her down; to have this over with, once and for all. To kill her. He stamped down on the accelerator, just as ferociously as he had on the brake, and his wheels spun in the snow before melting their way through and finally gaining enough grip on the road's surface to thrust the car forwards.

As he picked up speed, Colvin thought he saw, standing on the pavement to his right, Dylan the angel. He was there, and then he was gone. His rage subsided. This was madness! She had missed once; the wall had not got him. Now she was trying again, and he was falling for it. Once more his foot flew from accelerator to brake, as the car hurtled onwards. The woman looked startled, and made as if to move to one side, but not in time, as he struck her full on and instead of disintegrating into whiteness she crumpled beneath his metal with an impact that he felt reverberate through the whole vehicle; through his own body. The car lifted on its left side, as the front wheel rolled over her; it dropped and then raised again as the rear wheel followed suit, finally landing back down as he carried on away from the woman. He looked frantically in his rear-view mirror, and could see nothing but a spray of snow, thrown up by the wheels, in which there seemed a tinge of reddish pink.

He drove on.

It was some comparatively uneventful time later that he arrived at Dan Leno Walk and pulled up in front of the townhouse of Ms. Catherine Beauchamp.

He got out of his car, somewhat shakily at first, and walked to her door.

When she opened it, they said nothing. She simply stood to one side, and let him pass into her house; into her home; into her life.

Reminiscence (4)

S HE SITS, AND she waits. In her lap is a small black clutch-bag. Her hands grip it tightly.

She opens her eyes briefly, shuts them again, and remembers.

She remembered the pain. She remembered the sound of cracking, splintering bones as the car hit her full on; remembered the feeling of organs rupturing within her, of the spread of internal bleeding under her flesh, leaking out into the snow where that flesh was rent apart. Her last image, as consciousness fled, was of the snow she lay upon changing colour all around her to a strangely attractive, rosy pink. Her last thought: that even in this — as her body's flaming agonies overwhelmed her mind — death would be denied her.

The next thing she remembered was awaking in a hospital bed, surrounded by a gaggle of self-congratulatory surgeons and doctors, all proclaiming the miracle of her survival, the skill they had shown in mending her broken body. If she were not so wealthy — as indeed she still was, very much so — she would have wished for a pound for every time they told her that she should have died; that no-one, and certainly no-one of her age — *if only they knew* — should have survived such horrific injuries.

They did not know her name or address; she had nothing on her person to identify her. When asked, she claimed no living kin, which was true.

She feigned a degree of amnesia, and they christened her 'Mrs. Smith'. It stuck, for the duration of her long stay. Aliases or anonymity had always suited her.

Amongst all of her occult abilities, there was none which would hasten the regenerative process. She had learned to accept that the attainment of such skills was forbidden her, presumably as they would have enabled her to rejuvenate herself. She was never to be allowed to regain her youthful beauty.

Her painfully slow recuperation gave her a great many hours in which to think about things, although she could rarely curb impatience with her inability to take the fight, once more, to Simon Colvin. Oftentimes, she would curse her stupidity in underestimating him as an opponent. He may have appeared outwardly ineffectual, but she came to appreciate that he would not have been chosen lightly, without due consideration for the strengths needed to do battle with the powers of darkness at her disposal.

She had thought her timing perfect; had watched from afar (by supernatural means) the impending demise of his marriage, and had at the appropriate moment created just the climatic environment in which to capitalise on it — a relatively simple bargain made with certain elemental spirits — to catch Colvin at his weakest, play on that weakness and destroy him. So she had thought.

She had seen his car reverse away from the wall that should have killed him, and head towards her. She was too surprised by this twist of events, at first, to move. Then she thought she saw, standing on the pavement to her left, the angel. He was there, and then he was gone. By the time her attention returned to the onrushing vehicle, it was too late.

Now, even from her hospital bed, she was able to summon sufficient powers of divination to keep abreast of Colvin's movements, which had again taken an unexpected turn. She was uncertain, yet, whether this new addition meant he had a new ally she should be wary of, or a new vulnerability to be exploited.

Only time would tell.

She did know however, as the weeks and months of her recovery went on, that the pain of Colvin's loss — of his broken marriage — was diminishing, and without that inner turmoil he would be harder to manipulate.

She knew, all too well, how debilitating the loss of love could be…

✳   ✳   ✳

She opens her eyes briefly, shuts them again, and remembers.

She remembered losing the only person she ever loved.

Queen Victoria had been on the throne of the British Empire for more than forty years, when first she met her dearest Rose.

Her own fortune had allowed her to tour at will across the globe, and she was currently travelling through strife-torn Eastern Europe, secure in the knowledge of her safety from lasting harm.

Circumstance found her residing in rooms at the most famous gentlemen's brothel of those times, whose active life was still to last another dozen or more years, and whose repute would remain in the memories of many, well into the upcoming twentieth century. She had arrived in the city — itself, later, destroyed and all but forgotten — by railway from Vienna, and had sought where best to stay. The brothel, it seemed, was held in higher esteem than most hotels, and she had no qualms about requesting lodgings there. She was not the only lodger, and it was made very clear that she would not be expected to 'work' whilst in residence.

Almost immediately, she was befriended by the new madame of the establishment, who was thirty years her junior and younger than most of the employees, though nonetheless competent and highly respected for that.

This new proprietress, it was revealed by others, gave her Christian name to only a chosen few, and rumour also had it that no two confidantes had ever been told the same name.

When they did exchange such details, the soubriquet she was given was 'Rosemary', and she had no cause to question its authenticity. After all, she had not told the madame her true name either.

Of an evening, once the clientele were all duly catered for, Rosemary would often come to her rooms before retiring, to converse over a glass or two of claret for the day's remaining hours.

It was almost inevitable that they should become lovers.

No-one had ever touched her, not once, in all the years since that evening when the Devil had had His way with her; used her. She could not help but flinch when Rosemary's outstretched fingers first brushed her bare shoulder, as they sat on the edge of the bed together. It was very obvious that the contact had not been accidental. She apologised for her reaction, but her words were silenced with a fingertip, placed upon her lips. "Trust me," said Rosemary, her own lips pressing upon that same shoulder, as if a healing kiss upon a wound. This time, she did not jump. Her gown's gathered, puffed sleeves were gently pulled farther down her arms, and as more and more of her pale, hesitantly yielding skin was revealed, so it was kissed, until she was fully naked.

Then, under silken sheets, she was shown the kind of loving a woman can only give to another; a caring, sharing, wholly equal, beautiful loving. She was taught by the younger woman how to relax, how to react, and, in turn, how to give, and how to elicit response. There were no expectations, there were no demands. There was only respect, passion, joy; and a sweet, warm kindness born of a selfless loving which soon became love.

She had never known such sensations, such peace of mind, and when, after many blissful months, came the time for her to leave, to attend to business matters back in London, their parting was sorrowful, if tempered by promises of return.

A year later, return she did, and was able to repay what she saw as a debt — although Rosemary insisted there was nothing owed — in the only way she knew how: with sorcery.

She had arrived, unannounced, midway through one weekday morning, but could see immediately, despite Rosemary's unconditional pleasure at her reappearance, that something was troubling her friend; her lover.

"Rose, darling, what *is* it?" She had been pressing for an answer for some hours, during which they had luncheoned together, and gone on to make slow and tender love in Rosemary's own apartments.

Her face a picture of mock exasperation, unable to feel anger towards the other, Rosemary got up from their bed, went over to a dresser across the room and removed from it a letter. She stood, unashamedly nude, in the centre of the room, and read aloud:

> "My dear Fräulein,
>
> We are writing to advise you of the intended arrival at your establishment of our mutual client, the venerable undersigned gentleman, on the evening of the 18th of this month. We trust that you will afford him all due deference, and allow him to avail himself of the following services, which we have no doubt you can and will provide, for the appropriate remuneration, details of which are to be negotiated with these offices, and not under any circumstances with the gentleman in question.
>
> He requires the services of two young ladies, each of no more than nineteen years of age, to be made available to him, for an uninterrupted period of no less than four hours and no greater than twelve. One young lady is to be of Far Eastern origin; one of West Indian origin. One is to be large-breasted; there is no dimensional restriction in this regard; the other is to be wholly clean-shaven, excepting for the head. There has been no preference expressed, with regard to which young lady should bear which of the above characteristics. They will be expected to carry out any or all of the following functions, both willingly upon each other, and together with our mutual client…"

Despite having seen a great deal of every imaginable perversion in her comparatively few years, Rosemary found it impossible to read this man's demands aloud, and instead handed the paper over to her friend, who read the poorly quill-penned letter to its conclusion with a growing look of distaste and incredulity on her face.

It was signed for the purposes of authentication, both by the client himself, whom she recognised as a prominent British cabinet minister, in the city on political business, and by the man's solicitor, with express instructions that the letter itself be destroyed once its instructions were fully complied with.

"Are his requests as out of the ordinary as they seem?" she asked.

"Not individually," replied Rose, "but for just one customer it is unheard of. It's not even that which bothers me so much, though. This is not the first time he has visited us, and on the last two occasions my girls have ended up in hospital."

"I see. The eighteenth of this month, that is this coming Saturday. When do you have to reply to this?"

"Tomorrow evening, by way of a suitably cryptic telegram."

"Send it." An idea was forming. "Do you trust me, my dearest Rose?"

"Of course."

"Then send it, and let me provide the girls for you."

"You…" Rose had returned to the bed, a questioning frown on her face, but was silenced now with a fingertip, placed upon her lips, a graceful gesture, the significance of which did not go unnoticed by either of them.

"Trust me."

That was the first time she had ever attempted to raise a demon, and she had been doubtful if she possessed the skills necessary to summon two.

Fortunately, succubi and incubi were renowned for their eagerness to respond to being called upon, and she needed only a pair of the former; so much easier than raising one of each.

She left Rosemary's apartments for the remainder of that afternoon, and went to some of the less reputable quarters of the city seeking certain artefacts and substances which were required to be combined for the Summoning. She had read a great deal, over the years, on all matters supernatural, and knew well what was needed. She also asked for use of Rose's apartments, alone, on the coming Saturday evening, and that wish was willingly granted.

The weekend came around very quickly, and she hoped that she was ready. She had done all she could. Still, she was nervous. The anniversary of her annual 'payments' was fast approaching, and she was not sure, if this failed, whether she would get another, so deserving opportunity in time.

When everything was set, she stood in the centre of a darkened room, and tentatively closed her mind to all external interference. At the same time, she unfolded another layer of her thoughts, to allow them to reach out beyond herself, beyond the room in which she stood, beyond the Earth itself, into the highest reaches of Limbo, and she began to chant in a quiet, uncertain voice.

Hours seemed to pass, and still nothing happened. She doubled and redoubled her concentration, her efforts, and channelled her incantations, as if through a funnel, towards a narrower and narrower target, upon which she continued to focus all of her will.

Gradually, as the minutes, and then yet more hours passed, her confidence grew, and with it her voice, until the sounds that emanated from her throat seemed to fill the room, the world, the entire universe.

"Blood and souls," she finally cried. "Blood and souls for my Lord Lucifer!"

The air around her appeared to moan back, wordlessly, threatening to drown out her own desperate screams. Through closed eyes she could see an amorphous mass forming before her, and then another, next to the first.

Again. *"Blood and souls, my Lord! Blood and souls if you will aid me!"*

In her mind's eye now, she began to picture the shapes of the creatures she required, and knew that, as she did so, the masses in front of her took on those forms. She imagined their features, as she wanted them to look, and they were re-created perfectly by the two demons. As soon as she was content with their appearance, she began to create clothing for them; seductive, shimmering gowns. With the last of her energies she opened her eyes and beheld two stunningly beautiful young women, exactly matching the description in the solicitor's letter. She saw, also, the hungry, lascivious looks in these demons' eyes, and knew that she had succeeded.

"Go!" she shrieked, straining to hear her own voice over the growing turmoil around her. *"Do my bidding! Dispatch the one I direct you to! Go!"* Mentally, she focused the very last of her overstrained powers on one place; on one being. She felt the demons in front of her grow in size,

but not in mass, as they dispersed throughout the room and, at last, disappeared. All noise faded with them. Exhausted, she fell to the floor, unconscious from the demands of her efforts...

... and, some hours later, a vile, depraved man died a long-deserved, violent, wholly pleasure-free death.

Rosemary never asked her what part her friend had actually played in the man's death, which naturally had been hushed up by all parties concerned. The Press never said how he died, nor where, only that it had been of natural causes. Rumours abounded for a while though, among the streets of the city, of some far less than natural goings-on at the brothel that night — of horrific, unmentionable injuries — but these soon subsided, as such rumours are wont to do when replaced by other, newer scandals.

The lovers continued to meet, once a year, and their passion for each other never abated. Rosemary married, in time, and still they had their reunions, until Rose — *my dearest Rose* — grew too old and too frail to physically partake, and even then they corresponded regularly, until the time a telegram arrived, telling of Rose's death in a *Luftwaffe* firestorm just days before her ninetieth birthday.

Over the years, there had been other lovers, even long after her beauty waned. There had never been another love.

"My dearest Rose" was all she had said, as she read that telegram, and it was the closest she ever came to shedding tears.

Yes, she knew, all too well, how debilitating the loss of love could be...

✳   ✳   ✳

All this she remembers.

Still she sits. Still she waits...

BOOK THREE (The Beginning Of The End)

Give me these moments back
Give them back to me
Give me that little kiss
Give me your hand.

I know you have a little life in you yet
I know you have a lot of strength left
I should be crying but I just can't let it show
I should be hoping but I can't stop thinking
Of all the things we should've said
That we never said,
All the things we should've done
That we never did,
All the things that you needed from me
All the things that you wanted for me
All the things I should've given
But I didn't
Oh, darling, make it go away,
Just make it go away now.

Kate Bush
This Woman's Work

Chapter Nine (Yet Another Monday)

I T WAS DYLAN, the angel, who informed Simon Colvin that the
woman was still alive. They sat upon a park bench, not unlike
the one they had shared in Limbo, except that this was of earthly
origin, beside the Serpentine in Hyde Park.

The Summer sun warmed them, as Colvin was told of the injuries
the woman had sustained, and of her protracted recovery which had
kept her from continuing their conflict.

Nearly five months had passed since that unseasonally wintry day
on which so much had occurred. During that time, Simon Colvin and
Cathy Beauchamp had become what would commonly be referred to
as 'an item'.

She never had expressed any real surprise, upon his unannounced
arrival at her door, and seemed to take into her stride the absorption
of his life into her own living arrangements. She was unquestioningly,
selflessly supportive throughout the traumatic days of his possessions'
removal from his previous home, and seemed to know instinctively
when he wanted company, and when he was best left alone. She
had diplomatically fielded several abusive 'phone calls from Elspeth,
which had become far less frequent in recent weeks. As a couple,
they had grown very close, very quickly, and found that they shared a
great deal in common, including a love of travel, rock music, clothes
shopping, old movies, even children's books (and *Alice In Wonderland*

in particular) about which they could converse for hours… and often did.

Colvin had left Cathy on this particular August day, at the townhouse which they now shared, in order for her to get on with some writing undisturbed. A deadline loomed, and his presence was a distraction she could well do without whilst putting the finishing touches to a book review she was due to deliver the following day.

He was on a week's holiday from work, and had decided to take a lengthy stroll, lingering at its furthest point on the man-made banks of the Serpentine, where he had been watching the boating couples and families sculling to and fro with varying degrees of proficiency. It was a skill he had never mastered, and so watched purely out of interest, without criticism.

There was no reason for him to have taken his eyes from this scene, to glance some distance away to his left, but had done so when the urge suddenly came upon him, and seen Dylan walking along the wide, gravel-topped path towards him.

Now they sat together — their first meeting since Colvin had left the angel at Fulham Broadway Underground station — and there was a lot to be caught up on, for them both.

"How much longer?" asked Colvin, when their conversation returned from more general topics to that of his adversary.

"I gather she was discharged from hospital yesterday, and is as fully fit as she was prior to the… accident. I don't think we'll have long to wait before she next moves against you."

"Do we know what to expect?"

"How can we? She is capable of almost anything, natural or unnatural. All we know is that it must — if it hasn't already — soon involve this weapon I spoke of once before. We have since learned that the weapon itself is of supernatural origin, and will summon you to wherever it lies. Have you had any such intimations?"

"Would I recognise them if I had?"

"I believe so, yes. It's unlikely you'd be left in doubt."

Colvin thought hard, trying to recollect any recent, unanswered yearnings. "No," he said, "there's nothing I can recall."

"Well, if you do, you will let me know, won't you?"

"How? I've never known how to contact you. You just, well, *appear*."

"Think it. As you might expect, you are being pretty closely monitored as this thing progresses and, if you think it clearly enough, I'll know."

Colvin was particularly disturbed by this news, and said so. Just how much privacy did he actually have?

"All that you want or need," answered Dylan. "When I say 'monitored', it's not by any individual, as such, watching your every movement. It's as hard as ever to explain these things simply. Let's just say that certain types of thoughts on your part — certain signals — would ring… alarm bells, if you like, that I would be aware of."

Only marginally reassured, Colvin reflected instead on Dylan's greater grasp, during this visit, of colloquial phraseology. He was obviously still being tutored, and a lot better than he had been when they first met.

"Anyway," continued the angel, "I'm not tending to 'just appear' as often as I used to. The more time I spend on Earth, the more I've taken to walking from place to place. I found that, disappearing from one spot, and materialising in another, one misses so much… beauty."

Colvin looked around him, and could do nothing but wholeheartedly agree; after which neither of them spoke for several minutes while they took in the park's semi-pastoral scenery, marred only by the incessant din of traffic on the small but busy bridge across the boating lake.

It was Dylan who finally broke the silence: "How are things, anyway?"

"Things?"

"With your wife. With your children. With Mrs. Beauchamp."

Colvin decided, for the moment, not to correct either Cathy's marital status or her surname's pronunciation, and instead considered how best to answer the question. He certainly could not say it was something to which he had given little thought. One way or another, they were almost constantly on his mind — Elspeth, Sarah, Sam, Cathy — one, some, or all of them.

"Well," he replied, "I guess you could say that relations with Elspeth are, at best, *polite*." He emphasised the word, and hoped that he would not be asked to elaborate; that his multilayered meaning for the word would be fully construed. Dylan said nothing, but pursed his lips a little wryly.

"The kids are just great," continued Colvin. "They both had their birthdays last month, a couple of days apart. There was a party at their house, which I went… was invited to. Everything was just fine. I may have overdone the presents a little, but… well, you know. Then Father's Day, the month before that, that was hard. Their mother mailed cards for them, to my office, and…" He paused, clearing his throat. After a few moments, staring into the middle distance, he went on:

"I can't say they've been unaffected by what's gone on, but they're bearing up really well. I reckon adults put too much of their own angst onto expectations of how children will react to trauma. Kids — all kids — no, well, maybe *most* kids — are far more durable than we give them credit for; far more durable than we are.

"When *I* think of that day, when I left them, it still hurts like nothing else on Earth. It just takes your breath away; robs you of the will to do *anything*. And that pain never gets any less, either. It's just the gaps between which grow longer." He smiled, a little sadly, and then continued again, visibly brightening as he spoke.

"I've got them this week, you know, the kids. I'm picking them up this afternoon. It's a big occasion. Not only is it the first time I've had them for more than a weekend, it'll be the first time they meet Cathy. I think that's pretty good going, in just five months, don't you?"

"I can't really say," answered the angel honestly. "It's not something I've had much experience in. And I think one needs to have experienced what you mean, in order to understand what you're talking about."

"Then why did you ask?"

"Curiosity, I suppose, to a degree. But also, as you can imagine, a need to know how you're coping; whether you're ready for what's expected of you."

"Well, I'm coping as well as can *be* expected, and I'm as ready as I *can* be. Does that answer your question?"

"Not mine, Simon. My — my superiors…"

"Oh, yes, and how are the almighty powers that be?" Not for the first time, Colvin found himself relaxing into a bantering tone which belied the outlandishness of the conversation; enjoying the angel's discomfort.

Was that a little reddening of the cheeks he saw? Could an angel really blush?

Regardless, Dylan avoided rising to the bait. "So, how are things with... Cathy?"

Colvin felt rather guilty then, for having made his (*friend?*) — yes, his friend — so ill at ease, and he answered the question as simply and truthfully as he could. "Things with Cathy are really great, thanks. It would be wrong of me to say that I've never been happier, but I can safely say it's been a bloody long time since I was last this happy!" He grinned.

"I'm glad," said Dylan, and he was. "What are you all going to do together, this week?"

"I'm not sure yet. As I say, it's the first time all together, and the first *long* time ever. I started off just seeing the kids for one day every two weeks, and then that increased to weekends, but it was difficult without being able to bring them home to stay with Cathy and I. We had to stay at the empty flat of a friend of hers, who's away on a sabbatical, but that was far from convenient. Hopefully, things will work out much better now. The kids are on six weeks' holiday, and I have them for the whole of this one. One out of six ain't bad, I guess."

"I guess," echoed Dylan. He seemed genuinely pleased that things were improving in Colvin's life, and it was a pleasure not solely born of a need to know if the one person all of mankind's hopes were (unknowingly) pinned on appeared to be bearing up under the strain of his responsibilities.

"End of test?"

"Not quite, I'm afraid, Simon. Does Cathy know of your... task?"

"No. I haven't told her. I daren't. But I get the feeling I'm going to have to, and sooner rather than later. It preys on me a lot — I get lost in thoughts of what's to come — and it makes me kind of withdrawn at times. Not being able to explain, when asked what's wrong, it's something of a burden."

"I see. You think she won't believe you?"

"Dylan, *I* wouldn't believe me! Why should I expect anyone else to?"

"Do you love her?"

"Yes. I do."

"Does she love you?"

"She says she does."

"And you believe her?"

"Yes, of course."

"When love is such an intangible? Then why not let her decide whether or not to believe something else; something just as hard to grasp?"

"That's easy for you to say. You're not the one she's likely to have committed as a raving loony!"

"Simon, do you trust me?"

"You know I do."

"Then trust me when I tell you to trust Cathy."

Colvin was suddenly wary. "Do you know something I don't?"

Dylan looked at him then, very sternly, and for the first time the angel's beauty seemed overshadowed by an aura of near-limitless power. "I know more than you could ever begin to imagine."

Colvin simply nodded, convinced. Again, they said nothing for a while, until he felt ready to break the slightly uncomfortable silence.

"End of test?" He raised a quizzical eyebrow.

"End of test," said Dylan, and they both seemed much relieved.

"I have to go soon. I've got to get back, take the car and pick the kids up."

"The car. You had it repaired, I assume?"

"Yes. I told the insurers I hit a wall. Which was true. It seems I wasn't the only one to do so that day, in the bad weather." He went on to tell the angel some more of what had happened since leaving Elspeth and the children, but Dylan could see that it was upsetting him, so after a while changed the subject.

"Can I ask you one more thing?"

"Another test?"

"No, just something I've wondered about. When we first met, did our researchers really get it all *that* wrong; the 'music freak' stuff?"

Colvin laughed warmly. "Well, yes and no. As I think I told you before, I do like music, a lot, but I'm not a 'freak'. At least, I don't think I am. It's just that your facts were… well, wonky."

"Wonky?" It seemed that Dylan's colloquialism lessons had not yet covered slang.

"Awry. I don't know if it was by luck or judgement that you picked all things Woodstock for those key words of yours, but I was born the year after that movie and its soundtrack came out, and grew up with my parents playing little else. I learned to know almost backwards, but also to loathe, just about every song by every sixties' and early seventies' band or artist there was. When I left home, I vowed never to listen to another record, and took up collecting model soldiers, mainly because the military overtones pissed my parents off. Then after I... after I lost that collection, I started to get the urge to buy music instead. Don't ask me why. I guess I'm just an obsessive collector; it doesn't seem to matter of what. I then discovered that what my parents had tried to brainwash me with wasn't so bad after all, and was certainly a lot better than anything in the charts around that time. Elspeth hated it — hippy-dippy shit, she called it — so I never got to play my stuff very often. I do now. Does this make any sense?"

"A bit," admitted Dylan, suffering somewhat from excessive answer overload. "I've been doing a little more research of my own, you see, into some of your music. There was someone called Elvis Parsley. He was very famous, right?"

"Presley. Yes, he was famous enough, but for producing more turkeys than gems. If ever there was someone who should have died in some spectacular manner in 1959..." Colvin was on roll now, and Dylan began to reel from the barrage he had innocently unleashed. Regretting he had started the conversation in the first place, shocked also that Colvin could actually have wished somebody dead — a totally alien concept to an angel — and realising that the time for Colvin to pick up his children was fast approaching, he coughed and fidgeted, hoping to attract the other's attention, all to no avail, as the lecture continued: "... the same with your namesake, really. And then there was *Bohemian Rhapsody*, which I reckon is the last great rock 'n' roll record before punk came along and spoiled it all; but I've a friend who reckons it was the very antithesis of rock 'n' roll, and a death-knell for the genre..."

"Simon..."

"Mind you, punk wasn't *all* bad. There was *Never Mind The Bollocks*, which is great, and The Stranglers' first couple of albums…"

"*Simon!*"

"What? Yes, sorry, what? Did I get a little carried away? I do, you know." He was sheepish.

"A little. Haven't you got to be somewhere?"

"Huh?" Colvin looked at his watch. "Oh, shit! Yes. Look, I've got to run. It's been great seeing you again, Dylan. I'll… sorry… 'bye!" and off he took, at a half-trot, towards the nearest park exit where he would now need to catch a taxi back home, in order not to be late for his children.

Dylan stared after the rapidly receding form, a smile playing across his lips; then he rose too, and sauntered off, whistling, in the other direction. *Yes*, he thought. *End of test. He's ready, all right. A doddle.* It seemed the angel did know at least a little slang.

That night, Colvin and Cathy lay in bed together. She was asleep, and her shallow, peaceful breathing was a calming influence on his otherwise troubled mind.

He was wide awake, and could not shake himself of the notion that his life was being unduly manipulated by his so-called allies. He had gathered — but only because they told him so — that they could not interfere directly in Armageddon. Was that true? Did they actually control him far more than he knew? Had they, for some reason, manœuvred him towards ending his marriage? Had they, in the same way, brought about his meeting with Cathy; his being with her? Why? He looked at her sleeping form, watched the bed's covers fractionally rising and falling, and even wondered, briefly, if she were a party to the conspiracy. He dismissed this immediately, and swore at himself for allowing such a thought. He did not even know if there was a conspiracy.

Still, nagged an insidious voice, his own voice, deep within him, *what attracted her to you in the first place?* He tried to ignore the question; to subdue the answer, which rose unbidden into existence: *pity*. What sort of an attraction was that?

He tacked, purposely trying to change mental channels. Were these words — these doubts — being sown by his adversary? It would not be the first time she had put voices into his head.

He dodged again, sending his train of thought down yet another, far less disturbing route. The day had gone really well. He had been on time to collect the children, who had come to the house and met Cathy with a mixture of excitement and apprehension. In turn, Cathy had tried to be both low-key and enthusiastic, a tricky balancing act which seemed to have worked, as by the evening — and admittedly after a slow and occasionally shaky start — they were all chatting together quite cheerfully.

He and Cathy had previously discussed the idea of sleeping separately to begin with, until the children were used to the relationship, but he had felt that to be dishonest. So, when it came time for the children to go to bed, he had shown them the room they were to share, and had pointed out the adjacent room that was his and Cathy's, in case they needed him during the night. Apart from a small hesitation in Sarah's step, this revelation passed without reaction.

With these cheerier, increasingly fuzzy recollections jumbling his mind, Colvin eventually drifted off into a deep slumber.

He dreams: *a castle on a cliff a banquet a table a round table people around bespectacled arthur elspeth is mi'lady guinnevere bob dylan is lancelot elvis presley is the green knight cathy is morgana le fey in a loosefitting rather drab robe ginger baker he shouldn't be here should he is merlin sarah sam as pigs with fruit in mouths... west... fade...*

the castle in ruins cliffs awash with waves the banquet is over the entertainment begins lancelot and the green knight duet a medley of blowin' in the wind and heartbreak hotel segued via the operatic section of bohemian rhapsody backed by ginger baker he shouldn't be here should he on drums and now sly stone as the black knight on keyboards blowin' in the wind around the table is the wicked witch of the west... by the sea... fade...

toto i've a feeling we're not in kansas anymore stones sly stones all around bespectacled arthur carves pigs with a sword watched from a large rowing boat by morgana le fey and the wicked witch of the west... by the sea... camelot camelot camelot... it's only a model... shh... fade...

jeff bridges arrives as michael palin as sweet sir galuhad with the holy grail which is the sword which is excalibur the wicked witch of the west is melting i'm melting ginger baker he shouldn't be here should he is merlin is the wizard of oz follow the yellow brick road west… to the sea… to camelot… to tintagel… to TINTAGEL

"West!" He sits up, wide awake, his heart pounding in his chest. He shakes. Cathy holds on to him, calming him, soothing him, wiping his brow with her palm. With her other hand, she switches on a bedside lamp.

"It's okay, Simon. It's okay. Shh…"

Was it okay?

He closed his eyes, and tried to block out the confusion of images and sounds in his head. He was still shaking, but less so. Sweat poured from him, and chilled his skin despite the Summer night's balminess.

Making an effort to control himself, he wondered if his cry had awoken the children. It did not appear so. No sounds came from their room. Eventually he said, "I'm okay. Thanks, Cathy, I'm okay now."

"Are you sure?"

"Yes. Just a dream. That's all, just a bad dream."

"Do you want to talk about it? Do you remember it?" She was still concerned.

"No, I'm fine now. Go back to sleep."

"What's 'west'?" she asked, determined to be sure that he was genuinely all right; that he was not just saying so.

"Nothing. Go to…"

"Simon." She was insistent. "What's *'west'*?"

He looked at her then, and sighed deeply. "I have to go west, Cathy. *We* have to go west. Tomorrow." He glanced at the clock. It was past midnight. "Today."

"Today?" She could not help but be puzzled. "Where west?"

"By the sea," he said simply, still afog with the racing remnants of his dream, uncertain of his own assertions. "Cornwall, I think."

"Well, darling," she grinned, assuming he was joking, "that's pretty far west!"

"Camelot?" He seemed vague, incapable of stringing words together. He realised his confusion was unnerving her, and made an effort to be more coherent. "No. Tintagel. You, me and the kids; we have to get up and… and drive to Tintagel."

"Simon, that's *miles* away! It would take *hours*! Why there? Why now?"

"I don't know. It... it has to be. I'm not even sure I should be taking you. I should be going alone. But I can't leave the kids. Not with..." He trailed off.

"Not with me?"

"No, I don't mean that. I mean... not at all. It's the first time we've had them. I can't leave them. I can't leave you."

"Simon, you're worrying me. What's going on?"

Again, he looked at her. Again, he sighed. Dylan was right. Now was the time. "Do you trust me?" It was a question that had been asked of him so often, lately.

"Of course I do," she said. "You know I do."

"Then I've got something to tell you. It's not easy for me. It's not going to be easy for you. It's hard to explain. Shit, how many times have I heard *that* recently? I guess I'd better start at the start. But *where* do I start? I don't..."

"Simon." Her eyes betrayed a touch of fear now. Her voice shook a little. "Just tell me."

So, he just told her. Everything.

As he had once before, he found himself pouring out his heart to her in a rush which, once begun, could not be stopped until it was over.

Then, it was over.

He had begun with an hallucination — or what he had thought was one — of an angel at a railway station. He finished with a need to travel west, and a belief that he would find there a weapon; perhaps a sword. He left nothing out that had gone on in between.

They looked at each other, their heads close together on the pillows. They had lain back down, hands touching throughout, and he had spoken upward, towards the ceiling, afraid to look at her — to see her reaction — until he was done. Now, he was done.

Their eyes were locked together, and all he had left to say was, "Well?"

She took a long time before answering. Finally she spoke, quietly but firmly, without a trace of her earlier fear: "I don't *disbelieve* you, Simon. It's just that I can't believe you, either. Can you understand that?"

He let out a long breath then, which he had not even realised he was holding in, and he smiled. "Cathy, if you had said you believed me, I'd have thought you as mad as *I* sometimes feel."

She smiled back at him. "Then I guess we're off to Tintagel," was all she said. She made it sound like a family trip to the local supermarket.

He loved her, and he told her so. In the lamplight, her long, fine hair shone like burnished copper.

"You're not so bad yourself —" a pause, another smile — "for a madman." Looking over Colvin's shoulder at the clock, she whispered, "Darling, do we have to leave *just* yet?" She took his hand; placed it upon her breast.

"Corny," he said, "but cute." He, too, glanced over to check the time. "No. Not just yet."

fade…

CHAPTER TEN (The Battle For Something)

THE CAR JOURNEY westwards, on the M4 and M5 motorways, was as interminable as ever, if a little more bearable — less pungent, that is — after passing beyond the windward reach of the sewage farms alongside the former.

The children had objected somewhat to being awoken at four in the morning, and to being bundled into Cathy's estate car less than an hour later for a trip which seemed to have little to recommend it. Their initial interest in seeing a castle dissipated when they discovered that it was 'a castle that isn't there anymore'. Regretting the wording of his less than enticing description, Colvin tried instead to engage them in games that could be played along a motorway. Anyone who has ever done the same, in order to delay the inevitable cries of 'are we there yet?', will know how few variations on a theme there actually are.

Cathy joined in the alleged fun as best she could, but was hardly a practised hand, and was soon found by the children to be seriously lacking in the necessary offspring-entertaining virtues.

She did cause some amusement however, on the first occasion since meeting them that she called Colvin 'darling'. Their sniggering at this threatened to border on the hysterical, and she was bemused until Simon explained that he and Elspeth had never used pet-names for each other (aside from his shortening of her name to 'Ellie'). Thus, for some reason, the children found an endearment as traditional — not to mention, in their view, as soppy — as 'darling' well worth a giggle or two. Cathy turned around in the front passenger seat, to look back at Sarah, and stage-whispered that she called *all* of her men that, so she wouldn't get their names confused, and then she winked. Waiting for a response, she wondered if the concept — its obviously ironic falsehood — would be a little too mature for the eight-year-old, but she was met with a sneakily conspiratorial wink in return, and a bond was made.

A discussion followed, of names, pet-names, nicknames and the like, in an atmosphere of increasing hilarity, although Sam refused to be drawn on an epithet his friends apparently had for him in school, which seemed unknown even to his sister. Much was made of Cathy's surname, and its lack of written semblance to its spoken form. Jokes about powders and Places, though, were lost on the children.

Finally, the youngsters began to drift into semi-slumber, paradoxically exhausted by their lack of activity, and so their father took the time to reflect on just what was likely to be ahead of them once they reached their destination. Was this a fool's errand? Was he dragging them across the breadth of the country for no reason? Last night his dream had seemed all-consuming, its message obvious. Now, in the warm light of a Somerset mid-morning, he was far less certain of his objectives.

Deciding at the last moment — almost too late — to follow the slower, more scenic A39 coastal road from Bridgwater around to Tintagel, Colvin moved the car rapidly across several lanes and caused a furore of honking in his wake.

One vehicle, a large and self-important BMW, cut dangerously back across their path and slowed just in front of them with an irate display of brake lights, causing Colvin to do the same. It then sped off, back towards its intended direction, farther south-west along the motorway.

Colvin cursed loudly, and then glanced over his shoulder to see if the children still dozed. They did, but Cathy looked across at him in mock reproach. "Now, now, calm down, please… *darling.*"

"Fucking moron!" screamed the chauffeur, before turning and apologising to his passengers, not only for the profanity but also for veering across the road and slamming on the car's brakes so ferociously. He had only been doing this job for a week, and could not adjust to having fee-paying strangers in tow, nor help but feel proprietorial towards the brand-new BMW he had been given on his first day.

In the rear compartment, divided from the driver by an open, sliding glass partition, sat Sir Jeffrey Jones, Oxford don, historian, and the country's recognised authority on all things Arthurian. With him sat Professor Roxanne Wyatt, lecturer at CalTech Institute, metallurgist, and the world's recognised authority on Dark-Age and mediæval armoury. Despite the weight of their combined learning, they were actually discussing something not far removed from another conversation, so recently taking place in the car with which they had just had an altercation: they were debating the mispronunciation and misspelling of surnames.

"... and so when they called me," said Jones, "they asked me to confirm the spelling of my name, for the promotional material. I told them, 'Sir Jeffrey — with a "J" — Jones'. Look at what I received in the mail yesterday, too late to do anything about."

He reached into his briefcase, pulled out a small handbill and passed it across to Professor Wyatt:

"C.A.M.E.L.O.T.
Campaign Against Meddling in England's Love Of Tintagel

It is with the greatest pleasure that we announce our Special Guest for this Tuesday's Summer Fair at Tintagel Castle: the historian, Sir Geoffrey Whitherjay-Jones.

The proceedings will begin with a battle re-enactment, to take place in the fields between the outer Wards of the Castle and the Tintagel Parish Church of St Materiana.

This will be followed by an Exhibition, within the Castle Grounds, of arms and armour, on loan from the private collection of Professor Roxanne Wyatt of the California Institute of Technology..."

Jones's fellow passenger could not help but laugh. "Well, they got *my* name right." He did not look amused, and she continued her perusal.

> "… in one of two large marquees hired for the occasion. (In the event of inclement weather, refreshments will also be served therein.)"

It went on for several more paragraphs, describing the various festivities, including the professor's main reason for being there, the first public viewing of the famous Bossiney Sword. She finished reading, and then handed back the paper.

"Hardly the snappiest press release I've ever read," she grinned, still amused by the umbrage he took with his new-found misnomer. She thought it politic, then, to change the subject. "What do you know about the sword?"

"Very little, actually. I gather it was found by builders, a few years ago, on a site between Tintagel and Bossiney villages. It was buried quite deeply, well below some verifiably ancient remains, but no-one has been able to date it accurately, because it was nowhere near as corroded as it should have been. Do you have any idea why?"

"No, not for certain. The only expert I know personally who's examined it is Mulcahy, of Cambridge; d'you know him?"

"I think we have met, once, but not talked at any length."

"Well, he says the sword flies in the face of everything we know about arms from the period in which it seems to have been buried. The metals used are mixed in proportions unknown, in Europe at least, but which had already been discarded in favour of others in the Far East around two thousand years ago. He also said that the sword's too delicate — fragile, even — for use in battle; that it must have been ceremonial, or purely decorative. But sharp, apparently; incredibly razor-sharp."

"Its proximity to Tintagel," said Jones, "has set the Arthur nuts off again, of course, convinced it's Excalibur." He was always dismissive of his speciality's more romantic, legendary aspects, particularly as he had to continue to show an interest in them — even actively extol them — if he was to secure funding for more serious projects. "I only agreed to this afternoon's fiasco in order to meet you." He was hoping, before the day was over, to persuade her to collaborate on a book.

His flattery did not go unnoticed, but neither was it necessarily appreciated. The professor had only one thing on her mind: examining the sword; being the one — the only one — to prove or disprove its ancestry. If anyone could, it was she.

Jones continued, having accurately interpreted her thoughts: "Of course, it would not be prudent to expose it as a fraud, if fraud it proves to be, in front of our hosts and their guests, but I would be interested in knowing your opinions later… over dinner, perhaps." He was dogged.

"Perhaps."

"You know, I get so righteously sick and tired of all this magical sword tosh, don't you? Even this blade has been kept deliberately out of the public eye, by its owners whose land it was found on, with no other reason than to increase the mystique surrounding it. It really is the bane of my life…"

Whatever Sir Jeffrey Jones went on to say was drowned out by another blast on the car's horn, another tirade of abuse from the driver in response to some miscreant's incursion into their road-space, another unwarranted squeal of brakes, and the subsequent apology.

Would Jones have been heartened or horrified to discover that the sword they were en route to did, indeed, possess powers beyond any his limited imagination could ever have thought possible? Would such knowledge have kept him alive through the next twenty-four hours?

Simon Colvin, his children, and Cathy Beauchamp all arrived in Tintagel village a little before midday. He flatly refused to entertain the idea of staying anywhere too touristy, eschewing the likes of Pendragon House, the Camelot Castle Hotel, and especially the King Arthur Hotel (with accompanying 'Excali-bar' night club).

Instead they settled for a small, family-run guest house on the outskirts of the village. After commenting on the noise that abounded, they were told of the Summer Fair at the castle, and of the battle re-enactment, source of the ruckus.

Colvin had all but decided there were no grounds for an immediate trip to the castle, that his reaction to the previous night's dream had definitely been an *over*-reaction, and so he determined to enjoy this unexpected jaunt into the West Country for what it was, a holiday. He suggested lunch, before going to see the ruins, and there was a unanimous vote in favour from all concerned.

Trains did not go as far as Tintagel. At Bodmin Parkway station, a very elderly, white-haired woman, carrying nothing but a small black clutch-bag, disembarked from the most recent arrival and headed slowly, a little stiffly, towards where she could best find a taxi. She was discreetly observed by a youth, dressed in simple, blue denim jeans and a cotton T-shirt resembling an American football player's top.

Lunch at their guest house concluded, the Colvin/Beauchamp party took a leisurely stroll through the village, admiring dwellings and shops of varying antiquity, all roofed in moss-covered Cornish slate. As they walked, Simon Colvin told his children a little — what little he knew — of Arthurian legend, ably assisted by Cathy Beauchamp's greater knowledge — a writer's knowledge — of all things mythological. They illustrated their points with some of the tackier souvenirs in the gift shops that seemed to line the main streets.

As they drew close to the 'Island' — which, technically speaking, it was not — whereon lay the ruins of a castle rumoured to have once been fabled Camelot, the Summer Fair's re-enacted battle was drawing to a close.

Another — far more ferocious — was about to begin.

Colvin had also described to his children a little of what to expect when first seeing North Cornwall's world-renowned and turbulent surf — the best anywhere, some said — and so their initial view of Tintagel Island proved something of a letdown. The Celtic Sea was smooth and still, reflecting the cliffs' purple shadows, the cloudless blue sky, like a mirror.

Nevertheless, they paid their entry fee, walked through what was left of the ancient fortified gateway, negotiated the precipitous, rock-cut steps and crossed the modern bridge onto the island, where they wandered with other sightseers up and around towards the first of two large, striped marquees. There, an occasionally faulty microphone was being tapped at by a young studious-looking woman who began, less than confidently, to speak:

"Um, ladies and gentlemen, thank you... thank you for coming to our — um — little fair here, this afternoon. We certainly have some fine weather for it. Um, I hope many of you arrived early enough to see the battle re-enactment, which really was most spectacular. I think it will be a long time before any of us sees its like again. Anyway — um — without further ado, I'd like to introduce, and ask you to give a big hand for, our very special guest speaker, Sir Geoffrey Whitherjay-Jones." She began the applause, which was picked up and continued by people in the audience, many of whom were in total ignorance of whoever had just been introduced.

Sir Jeffrey Jones came up onto the makeshift podium and, with a pained expression, thanked his hosts for inviting him. He went on in turn to introduce Professor Roxanne Wyatt — who joined him and sat down (on a chair which had to be hastily produced from somewhere) just to the left of where he stood — before beginning his prepared speech.

"Welcome to Tintagel. For those of you who have not been here before, Tintagel's bay, as you can see, is small and walled by high, bleak cliffs, a natural subject for romantic painters and poets of the past two centuries. Most of the castle ruins stand on the inland cliff — past which you walked on your way to this marquee — but some are on the west cliff, which is a narrow promontory now crumbling dramatically into the sea and carrying the ruins with it.

"In the very dry Summer of 1983 there was a disastrous fire, affecting about one third of the summit of the island and spreading to the lower terrace behind us, opposite the mainland. Fortunately, much of the damage from that time, to the island's flora and the like, has since been restored.

"But most of you, of course, are here because of the island's links with King Arthur. It was Geoffrey of Monmouth, and his fabulous *Historia Regum Britanniæ*, or *History Of The Kings Of Britain*, published around 1139, who sowed the more romantic seeds; that the palace belonged to Gorlois, Duke of Cornwall, whose beautiful wife Ygerna aroused the love of King Uther Pendragon. Uther besieged Tintagel and then, aided by the magician, Merlin — whose 'Cave' is beneath our feet as I speak — was changed into the semblance of Gorlois, made his way secretly into the castle at night and seduced Ygerna, who subsequently gave birth to Arthur…"

Simon Colvin's arm was around Cathy's shoulder, and he felt her shudder. It was then that he noticed how dramatically the temperature had fallen. Sarah and Sam were tugging on his other arm, bored with the lecture and asking to explore more of the island.

They went outside, and found that the sky had become an angry, cloud-filled slate-grey. The white stripes of the marquees glowed a sickly yellow in the peculiar half-light. At the children's insistence, they walked past (and dropped a few coins into) the old well, moving on from there as close as Colvin felt was wise to the edge of the now windswept cliff. It dropped almost sheer to the sea which was pounding — turquoise, green, sapphire, violet; spread with clear, lacelike foam — into the sharp rock-cleft where it ran with savage force, sending huge clouds of spray to lick the wet, black rocks above.

Suddenly, no more than a hundred yards out to sea, a lightning bolt struck the water's surface and set it to boiling for an instant. The children screamed, then laughed, and the two adults jumped and backed rapidly away from the cliff's edge. A cold, stinging rain began to pelt them, and they all ran for the shelter of the closer, second marquee. Its sides billowed, but it showed no signs of being dislodged from its pitch.

As they entered, another giant spark flew from sky to sea.

"Simon, it's awful," cried Cathy. "Oh, God, I hate storms! I always have. Since I was a child…" Another, closer thunderclap made her scream out this time, and she clung to him, plainly terrified. He knew nothing of this fear of hers; had no cause to have known. He held her tightly.

The children were half-scared, half-fascinated by the raging weather, as they stood at the verge of the shelter which the marquee provided and peered out. Simon and Cathy were further inside, in semi-gloom as there was no artificial lighting switched on yet. He was torn between comforting Cathy and joining his children; pulling them back into the comparative safety of the darkened tent. It would offer no protection if lightning struck, of course, but then neither did anything else nearby.

Cathy literally shook from head to toe with fear, and seemed in danger of losing her self-control. If the children noticed, would it make them panic too? Reluctantly, he led her over to a chair, barely visible through the murk, and explained that the children should not see her like that; she understood, but could do nothing about it.

"Go to them," she said, through gritted teeth. "I'll be fine. Just leave me here…" Another crash, nearer still, and she buried her head in her hands.

Colvin was halfway between Cathy and the children when a huge spear of white and yellow fire roared to earth just outside the marquee. It illuminated the interior for a fraction of a second, and the urge he had to run to his children drained from him. Imprinted in negative on his eyes were two things: a long, slender sword, suspended in mid-air by cords hung from the ceiling, and an old woman's silhouette, just below it, looking upwards. Then darkness returned, and with it the need to rescue his children. He looked towards the tent's entrance, but they were gone.

In the gloom, he heard the old woman's voice. "A sword," she said. "I sought a cup. The one true Grail takes many forms, I was told. The sword?"

Almost as if this were a command, the weapon itself began to emit a low hum; a warm light, dim at first, but growing in strength, shone from it; from within it, and a sweet smell of roses filled the area around them. The woman reached up and touched the sword, which seemed to shriek louder and bucked on its cords. She snatched her hand away, as if burned, then turned to face Colvin, snarling at him, her face livid. "Damn you, Colvin, you'll not have it!" She reached into her clutch-bag, pulled out a small kerchief, and with this in hand grabbed again at the sword, yanking it from its bindings. Keeping the weapon before her, its point towards Colvin, she rounded him and moved towards the exit, where the storm still bellowed. She retreated, out and to the side of the marquee, and this galvanised Colvin into action — but what action to take? He knew that so much depended on wresting that sword from the woman, but he had to find his children. He looked at Cathy, who still sat, head in hands, seemingly unaware of what was going on around her, and he ran outside…

… straight into someone running inside. It was Dylan, the angel. "Simon! Go after the woman. I'll look after the others!"

His adversary could just be seen, slipping into the first marquee. He left Dylan, and pursued her.

Cathy Beauchamp could hear nothing but the storm. It tore at her nerves, shredding them. *Simon, Simon, Simon…* Over and over in her head she called to him, begged him to help her; knew that he could not. *Oh, darling, make it go away,* she implored. *Simon, Simon, Simon…* There was a tap on her shoulder; she jerked her head up, out of her hands, and saw a young man who could only be described as nothing less than beautiful, with stunningly bright blue eyes.

"Quickly," he said, "come with me."

"What?" She couldn't move; could not go out into the horror ripping down at her from the skies. "No! Who the hell are you?"

"Dylan, a friend of Simon's." He seemed to mumble something else, which she could not catch, and there was suddenly silence outside. "Come, there's no time to waste. The children are safe. I have them…"

"Dylan." The name was familiar, and then it came back to her. "The angel?"

"Yes." The urgency in his voice grew. *"Come on!"*

"No." She could not believe this. Not now.

She saw impatience in his eyes, but not anger, as he backed away from her. Before she knew what was happening, he shook his shoulders, as if dislodging an unwanted load from them, and there behind him was a pair of golden wings. She looked down, and saw that he hovered a foot or so from the ground. *"Now* will you come!"

Her chin hanging loose — inarticulate, questioning noises caught at the back of her throat — she rose and followed him, in a dream, from the tent. Outside, things were no less extraordinary. People were running from the other marquee, but she quickly saw that they were not running at all. They all held poses of fleeing from something or someone, but none of them actually moved. Like statues, they were frozen in mid-flight. Even the rain had stopped. It was in the air; they moved through it, but it no longer fell. "How…?" was all she could manage, before the angel grabbed her arm and began hurrying her towards another, higher point on the island, which seemed shrouded in a dense, almost impenetrable fog.

Dylan slid between Cathy and this peculiar phenomenon, muttered something under his breath, and it cleared to reveal a set of railings around an opening into the ground. Behind this fence were the children, yelling at her to come to them.

He helped Cathy through, followed her, and the mist closed in again around them. She stared at the angel. "How did you *do* that?"

"Shh... it's a kind of magic," he said, winking. Despite the urgency of the moment, he could not help thinking: *hey, a pop-culture reference; Simon would be proud of me*, before hastening them all down into the tunnel at their feet.

They descended a short way, and stopped halfway between their entry point and an exit at the other end of the tunnel.

"What now?" asked Cathy, desperately clinging to the terrified children, who hung as tightly back on to her.

"Same again," he said, standing between them and one of the side walls. The next moment, there was a ragged-edged opening through to a set of rough-hewn steps downwards. "Not even the trustees of the castle know of this way down," he told her. "It was closed off at both ends hundreds of years ago. It will lead you down to the cave. Stay there. Simon and I will find you. I'll close the opening after you."

As Cathy and the children raced through, they felt the gap shutting behind them. As it did so, Cathy heard Dylan call out one more thing, but she could not tell if it was 'Be sure to hide' or 'Beware the tide'. They descended.

In the first marquee, Simon Colvin and the woman circled each other warily, moving in and out of a forest of mannequins, all set in the startled positions they had assumed when an old woman wielding a sword had entered the tent from the storm beyond. On the podium, Sir Jeffrey Jones seemed caught in mid-exclamation, his unmoving body half-turned in the direction of the seated Professor Wyatt.

It was towards this dais that the two enemies edged. The woman seemed weary, as if her exertions tired her. She moved gingerly, and Colvin remembered that she had only just come out of hospital; that she must be feeling the effects of her long recuperation. This gave him hope, until he realised that, with the sword, which still wailed like a siren, still glowed an eery gold, she was all but invulnerable.

At that moment, she swung the weapon in a wide, sweeping stroke, and he barely managed to jump back to avoid it, stumbling against the raised edge of the podium as he did so and falling onto it. The next swing came from over her head, in a downward arc aimed at his prone body. He rolled to one side, and the blade bit deeply into the timber base. She tugged at the sword, which seemed reluctant to be released, giving Colvin time to rise, mount the dais and move closer to the immobile figures there; props on a makeshift stage.

The sword came free, a thwarted yell escaping it; the woman staggered backwards against a central wooden pole, from and around which the marquee was erected. Undeterred, she came at Colvin again, and swept the weapon at him once more. He dodged behind the statue that was Sir Jeffrey Jones, and the sword seemed to pass right through the peer's midriff without effect.

Colvin jumped from the back of the podium, and ran around it towards the centre of the tent. Again the woman turned, with a speed that belied her years and apparent frailty, and she lunged at him. He backed into the central pole, and she stabbed again. He moved to one side, but not quickly enough. The sword pierced his upper arm, clean through and deep into the wood on the other side. He was pinned into place, pain flaming outwards from the wound as the woman struggled to release the blade. Gathering all of his rapidly waning strength, Colvin pulled his leg up, placed his foot against the woman's stomach and kicked her backwards. She fell against the stage, temporarily stunned. With his free hand, he too pulled at the sword but it was immovable. The woman sat up, dazedly glaring at him, cursing him, and without thinking he turned as if to run. He screamed then, as the agony in his arm doubled and enveloped him, but suddenly he was free of the central pole. The sword fell at his feet, and he grabbed it before running out of the marquee, blood beginning to pour from his wound. Looking at the sword he saw that it had snapped, its point left embedded in the pole. He sped wildly around the back of the marquee, but found nowhere left to go from there; only the void beyond the cliff, and death on the rocks below. He wondered what had happened to his children — and to Cathy — and then the woman came around to face him.

She said something he could not hear, pointed at him, and he was thrown onto his back, knocked flat as if by a blow. He rose to his knees, she spoke again, and again he was floored; being pushed inexorably up the slope towards the cliff-edge. One last, sorcerous shove, and he would be gone.

She shoved. He slid, over the edge and down...

... onto a small ledge, a rocky terrace ten or fifteen feet below the cliff-top. He landed hard on his damaged arm, and blacked out for a second from the increased pain. Coming to, still holding the broken sword, he scrambled close to the cliff-face and eased his way around, until he found a small natural cave created by an overhang. Here he hid, panting, passing helplessly in and out of consciousness.

Above him, the woman peered over the edge of the cliff and saw nothing but a steep grassy drop to the sea below. She smiled. Colvin was dead. She had succeeded. Slowly, and in not a little pain, she began to walk away, down towards the bridge onto the mainland.

In 'Merlin's Cave', far below, the children, resilient as ever, played in a sea that did not move, whilst a still-shaken Cathy looked on, her back to rocks which had re-formed behind them after opening from the secret steps. Believing they had been saved only from a storm (which now seemed over) — knowing nothing of what went on above — the children's fear had been overcome by their fascination with waves that hung motionless in mid-air, that they could walk through with neither a splash nor a ripple being caused. They laughed. They frolicked. Cathy, stunned beyond imagining what further dangers their noise might arouse, just watched them.

Colvin awoke from a doze. At first he thought Cathy shook him awake, in bed, at home, but then his injured arm flared up and reminded him of where he was, and why. Dylan stood over him.

"Simon, come on, get up. We've got to reach the others."

"Cathy! Sarah! Sam!" All was suddenly very real. "Where are they?"

"Safe, but I don't know for how much longer. I can't sustain slowed time any more, and we need to get to them, before the sea does."

The angel helped Colvin to his feet. As he did so, the wind picked up, the rain lashed them, and waves crashed. Above, they heard an almighty scream. Below, they heard another.

Cathy only closed her eyes for a moment. She was so tired. When she opened them again, it was to see Sarah and Sam disappear beneath a wave that had burst into life around them, engulfing them. She screamed.

The wave flattened out, racing towards the far end of the cave which went right through the neck of the island, and she saw Sam bob to the surface. Sarah did not appear, and in seconds the boy was also resubmerged by the next wave. Without thinking, Cathy dived headlong into the raging torrent, and flailed blindly about, hoping to make contact with one or both of the children. Sucking down a mouthful of salt water, she gagged, but continued to feel around her. She heard a shout and saw them, tumbling on the crest of the next wave which crashed down upon her. Somehow she found and clung on to them both, desperately turning Sarah head-upwards in her arms, struggling to hold all of their mouths free of the water. Another onslaught spumed around them, tossed them, threatened to drag them under and out to sea. Yet another threw them against rocks and dazed Cathy, but still she held tightly to her charges. Out into the centre of the narrow channel again, and back onto the rocks. Again. Again. The next time, she knew, would be the last. She could hold on no longer. The three of them hit the rocks, and as her senses left her she felt the children wrested from her grasp by the murderous sea. It dragged at her too…

… dragged her upwards and out of the water, onto the rocks themselves. She coughed; salt water was expelled painfully from her lungs. Through half-focused eyes she saw Sarah and Sam on the rocks beside her, the sea beneath them all. She saw hands, strong male hands, checking pulses, nursing bruises. She looked up, saw Simon, and Dylan the angel, and passed out again, this time with an exhausted smile on her battered lips.

A short time earlier — just before Colvin and Dylan descended to the cave and found the others, helping them ashore — in the first marquee Professor Roxanne Wyatt turned to where someone had pointed, indicating an old woman with a sword. She looked, but saw no-one, only the storm raging outside. She turned back to Sir Jeffrey Jones, in time to hear his "I say!" and have his severed torso tumble into her lap. Blood erupted from the clean-cut plateau atop his hips, before his legs buckled and landed at her own feet. She screamed.

REMINISCENCE (5)

S HE SITS, AND she waits. In her lap is a small black clutch-bag. Her hands grip it tightly.

She opens her eyes briefly, shuts them again, and remembers.

She remembered the long journey home by train, spent imagining what it would be like to die, a peaceful, natural death, now that her task was completed.

She had waited until she returned to her apartments, before using her powers of divination to spy on the remains of Simon Colvin. She had not intended to gloat; it was merely to be sure.

Her cry was one of disbelief, frustration and sheer, blind fury. He lived! How? They all lived. Were they charmed? She looked again, and saw the angel. Now she knew.

Now she knew, also, how time that day had been halted.

She saw they had already begun driving back to London, all together.

Looking further afield, she turned her second sight towards Tintagel. Police were now present, in great numbers, and she viewed the cloven body in the marquee.

She was shocked. Despite all the death she had seen in her life — all that she herself had caused — this was the first time she had killed someone who was not in payment for her damnation; her first truly innocent victim. It took her breath away.

The images in her mind began to waver, and she refocused her mental efforts, concentrating, not letting the man's death prey on her. This was all Colvin's fault. He would pay, dearly.

In the marquee, a policeman picked at the central pole with tweezers, extracting tiny slivers of metal from a gash therein, placing them in a small polythene sachet.

Having seen all she needed to, she had looked instead, then, into her open clutch-bag; the sword-point was still lying there. Was it really a part of the Grail?

✸   ✸   ✸

She opens her eyes, and her clutch-bag, briefly; then shuts both again, and remembers.

She remembered the first V.I.P. she had ever killed, the cabinet minister in Rosemary's brothel. The man in the marquee had been her last, but there had been many in between.

Whether it was a peculiar strain of cruelty on her part, or a need to test how far she could push the limits of brazenness without repercussions, or perhaps a mixture of both (she was never sure), there was no denying that political killings, particularly in America where such things were more easily arranged and carried out, had become an occasional feature of her annual payments.

She had tried, whenever possible, to make the subjects those who were most deserving — whose crimes far outweighed her own — although she had to concede a degree of pettiness when it came to the Kennedys.

At a social gathering in London, around the outbreak of World War Two in Europe, she was maliciously insulted in public — even now her mind refused to trawl up the sordid specifics — by Joseph Kennedy and his wife Rose (an affront to her lover's name), and so went on to take a ruthless and wholly selfish revenge on their male offspring over the next thirty years. First and easiest to arrange was Joseph Jnr.'s demise during the War, followed by John in 1963 and then his younger brother Robert five years later. She had tried and failed to take down their youngest brother and rottenest apple, Edward, as he escaped the Massachusetts car 'accident' which should have proved fatal. That was the first and only time she had employed a different agency from the one she normally used to hire whichever undesirables would carry out such work for her in America.

At around the same time, she had also been responsible for the assassination of Malcolm X, one of the few actions she subsequently came to regret. Her attempt to redress the balance, with George Wallace in 1972, proved fruitless; and that, combined with the earlier, unsuccessful attempt on the youngest Kennedy son, had made her recall the Devil's proviso, so many years before: "... you will be denied — though you'll seldom realise it — any already promised either to Myself or to God, and whose purpose is as yet unfulfilled." She had often wondered, with regard to her few failures over the years — such as Ford and Reagan (she had acquired a taste for presidents) and, probably her most perverse excursion into attempted assassinations, Pope John Paul II — to which deity they had actually been promised.

She had rarely experienced even a trace of guilt over her actions, nor over the fate of some of the poor unfortunates she manipulated or paid to do her bidding. Had such cold-heartedness always been a part of her, or did it become an inherent trait of all the soulless damned?

Likewise, she had never considered arrest or imprisonment a possible outcome of her actions. Damned she might be, but also was she charmed, and had seemingly managed always to avoid capture, without even realising it threatened or was imminent. Had it ever really been close? Ignorance (of some things), it was said, was bliss, and with this she could only wholeheartedly agree.

⛤ ⛤ ⛤

She opens her eyes briefly, berates herself for allowing her mind to wander — now, more than ever, she needs to concentrate on the task at hand — shuts them again, and remembers.

She remembered seeing that Colvin and his woman, their brats, and the angel were all driving back towards London.

She thought again of the man — the innocent man — killed in the marquee at Tintagel. Her need to destroy Colvin up until that point had been a purely clinical one; a means to an end. Now it had become a deep-felt, personal hatred; one she would give vent to, upon them all. That unnecessary, unwanted death — her persistent failures, her frustrations — they were the fault of Simon Colvin, but she would make them *all* pay, dearly. Their deaths, when they came, would not be pleasant.

She had looked then — her stare fixed upon its ornate face for several minutes, watching their seconds tick by — at the large, seventeenth-century Tompion chronometer (bought when such things did not cost a king's ransom to procure). It sat on the high mantelpiece over an open fire that roared in the grate and which, despite the present mid-Summer heat, had failed to warm her. She gauged how long it would take them to return to the city.

If she began right away, she would just about have time enough to get everything ready. She would strike again, while they were all still at their weakest.

It was time, once more — *the last time?* — to beckon a demon from the heart of Limbo.

Then she had begun to prepare for the Summoning.

✯   ✯   ✯

All this she remembers.

Still she sits. Still she waits…

Chapter Eleven (Yet Another Tuesday)

I t was hard to believe that it was still the same day, so much had happened.

Twenty-four hours earlier, Simon Colvin had sat in Hyde Park planning a week's peaceful quality time with his children. Now he, they, and the woman he loved had all nearly been killed three hundred miles west of that park and the comparative sanity of London.

They had remained on the rocky higher ground of the cave beneath Tintagel Island, clear of the still-churning sea whilst Cathy and the children recovered from their ordeal at the mercy of its ferocious depths.

All three of them seemed to have violently expelled more than enough sea water to fill a small swimming pool.

Above, they could hear the approaching sirens of emergency vehicles. Colvin directed an enquiring glance at Dylan, the angel, whose replying nod was one of reassurance. When a handful of uniformed police came down to the beach — what little of it was accessible — and peered into the cave, Dylan motioned the group to stillness and, despite being in open sight, they went unnoticed.

This supernatural invisibility aided them in their subsequent ascent back up the cliffs, away from the castle's grounds and through the village, on which the sun shone brightly once more, towards the guest house. Very few words were exchanged along the way; all were too exhausted,

shocked, or both, to converse. Colvin still clung to the broken sword —
which was quiescent now — with the hand of his good arm, his injured
one limp at his side. The children each held one of Cathy's hands as they
walked.

Once all back in their room, a hot bath was run for the children,
and whilst they soaked Dylan examined Simon's wound. He was able
to ease some of the pain it caused, but not actually to heal it. Blood
had congealed around the clean-cut entry and exit points though, and
stopped any more from seeping forth.

Next, Dylan turned his attentions to Cathy, whose body was an all-
over mass of bruises and abrasions. These were more easily soothed by
Dylan's magical touch, although Simon could not help the green mood
that plagued him while he watched, fidgeting all the while. Cathy soon
noticed this, and found his reaction amusing; helping to break the overall
air of tension which lessened as the other two joined in her laughter.

The angel then went into the bathroom, coming out some time
later and saying that the children, too, were fine now. Their wounds,
on younger, suppler skin, had virtually disappeared, and he had also
managed to erase their memories of all but the most prosaic of the day's
events. They remembered visiting the castle, sheltering from a storm,
and getting soaked by the rain when they left the marquee's protection.
Their father's injury was due, they believed, to his having slipped and
fallen whilst running after them. Cathy's wounds were less obvious,
and would not give rise to comment.

She was the next to take a refreshing soak, followed by Simon who,
when he later emerged from the bathroom, saw that the children had
both fallen asleep on top of their beds, and that Dylan and Cathy sat
talking quietly. The angel had long since dispensed with his purely
ornamental wings — he seemed to use them only for effect, when
needing to convince someone of his powers — but she was no less
awe-struck at being in his presence, and took a writer's opportunity to
quiz him thoroughly. Despite his subtle evasiveness around a few of her
topics, he answered as fully and truthfully as he could.

"... no, Cathy, ghosts are not angels. The spirits of the dead are
entirely different beings. Angels are not born; neither do we die. We
just, well, *are*."

Simon looked at Cathy in mock scorn. "Don't you even know *that?*" His pretended insouciance at being around supernatural entities was deliberately less than convincing, and reduced them again to mirth.

Careful not to disturb the children, their discussion turned to what was to happen next. "I think," said Dylan, "it's safe to assume that the woman will have to rest now. There will be a respite before the next onslaught."

"But for how long?" asked Colvin. "And do we stay here, or return home?"

"I have a feeling the next round will be in London. The farther away the woman is from certain artefacts she must surely keep at home, which aid her powers, the weaker she is. Now that you have the sword, she will need all of her resources if she is to stand a chance of besting you."

"And what *are* her chances?" asked Cathy.

"Still good. The sword helps, but will not make Simon invincible."

"What *is* the sword?"

"I'm still not wholly certain, but I'm beginning to get the impression that it's one manifestation of a very powerful object indeed."

"But it's broken."

"Its power, Cathy, is not in its strength as a weapon, but in the influence it exerts on those who come into contact with it."

"Do you mind," requested Colvin, "if we keep to the matter at hand, and save the metaphysical speculation for later?"

"Sorry," they said, in unison.

"So, we return to London, right?"

Dylan thought this best, and it was decided that they should leave straight away. Colvin was in no position to drive with only one fully functioning arm, and so the duty fell to Cathy who, together with the angel, carried the still-sleeping children out to the car.

The drive back was uneventful. The children slumbered on. The others talked for a while, and then fell silent while the miles rolled relentlessly by.

Night had fallen, and no-one had spoken for almost an hour, when Colvin leaned forward in his rear seat between the children and tapped Dylan on the shoulder. "What are you looking so pleased about?"

"What do you mean?"

"For ages now you've been craning your neck from side to side, peering everywhere and grinning like the Cheshire Cat. What's up?"

Dylan chuckled. "Well, apart from having no idea what a Cheshire cat is, it's really quite simple. I've never been in a car before, and it's *fascinating!*"

The others were amazed and amused by this, in equal measures, but soon realised they had no right to be. While Dylan could do and show them things so otherworldly they defied belief, he, in turn, with little or no earthly experience, found the most mundane, everyday things just as astonishing. That a simple car journey could induce such childlike wonder in their immortal companion endeared him all the more to them.

This kick-started their conversation again, as Dylan explained that angelic visitors were not really so uncommon on Earth, though many tended to blend in a little more subtly — be somewhat better adapted to their situation — than he. "There's a quote from a version of your Bible that sums it up quite well: 'Do not forget to entertain strangers, for by so doing some people have entertained angels without knowing it'."

Cathy then asked a question, though she was at a loss to find a reason for the others' hilarity when she began it with, "What I don't understand is this...

"If you've quite finished, the pair of you! Dylan, how come you were able to help us out back there, at the castle? I thought you and your kind couldn't intervene in what's happening."

"I can't — in fact, I didn't — not directly. I slowed time to a virtual standstill, but that was in an attempt to avoid... what are they called, now... civilian casualties, is it? Yes. And then I helped you and the children to safety, and Simon to rescue you all from the sea, but at no time did I actually assist Simon in his fight with the woman. The rules are very precise about what can and can't be done."

"Rules?"

"Oh, *don't ask!*" exclaimed Colvin. "You really don't want to know." He glared at the angel's back, though with no real malice.

Cathy glanced in the rear-view mirror and, in the limited illumination offered by other cars' headlights, was able to see Simon and the children in the back. "Poor darlings," she said. "I never should have let them go into that sea."

Simon's "Don't be so silly" and Dylan's "Nonsense" overlapped in their eagerness to reassure her. The angel was most insistent: "Cathy, you were very — incredibly — brave. No-one could have asked more of you. It is not, after all, your fight."

She turned her head then, to look at the angel full on. "Oh, yes, it is."

"No. It cannot be. Not only is it too dangerous, it's not allowed. This must be between Simon and the woman, and no-one else."

"You really think it's that simple?"

"It has to be."

"Then it seems to me that Heaven is far more out of touch with humankind than it has a right to be. How can you expect me *not* to get involved?"

Dylan could not answer her. Instead he became very quiet, withdrawn, while he pondered these newly arisen complications, and it was up to Colvin, once again, to break the ensuing silence.

"We're taking the children home." The others, unsure of his meaning, waited for him to elucidate. "Look, we nearly died today; *they* nearly died, and I can't put them in any more danger. I know you said there will be a gap now, while the woman rests, but I can't afford to take any chances with the kids' lives. Cathy, pull in to the next service station. I'm going to call their mother. We're taking them back to her. I want them safe."

Elspeth was less than happy. She had no problem with getting the children back early, but was furious with Colvin for taking them on such a long journey without her knowledge; for putting them at risk in a place where even he had fallen and hurt himself. If he was injured, so might they have been. It was unacceptable.

Colvin was suitably contrite, and all was finally agreed; the children were returned safely home just before midnight. They had slept through the whole journey.

CHAPTER TWELVE (Ring Of Bright Fire)

YLAN WAS ADMIRING Cathy's prodigiously print-lined living-room walls. Every traditional and contemporary style was displayed there, although the greatest emphasis leaned towards the more avant-garde. There were a couple of original Onos that particularly impressed him.

Despite the lateness of the hour — it was almost two in the morning — and the humans' physical exhaustion, none of them seemed inclined to call an end to their long day.

Simon and Cathy shared a bottle of red wine and some *hummus bi tahina* with Doritos, all of which the angel declined.

As they finished their snack, Colvin went over to the C.D. racks, scanning the discs' spines for something to play. He selected one, and slotted it into the player. Cathy glanced up in surprise at his choice — it was one of hers; Juliette Greco — but he merely shrugged, smiled, and sat back down next to her, taking her hand.

Everything seemed relatively normal, and it took a while for them even to notice the sound.

It was a buzzing, seemingly far away, like that of bees heard across a meadow. It attracted no more than raised, enquiring eyebrows to begin with, but after some minutes became more noticeable; more urgent.

"What *is* it?" asked Cathy.

Realisation was slow in coming, and struck Colvin first. "The sword!"

It was still in a bag, in their bedroom, and he ran to fetch it before unzipping the top and unleashing a noise and a near-blinding light, both undoubtedly of warning.

Dylan looked around them, and began to sniff the air in an almost feral way. His eyes were questing, desperate to locate something which, at the same time, it was obvious he hoped not to find. Suddenly he stood stock-still, rigid, and stared at the other two. "No," was all he said.

For the second time in as many minutes, Cathy asked "What *is* it?", but this time the mounting fear in her voice was all too evident.

"She can't," said the angel. "She wouldn't."

"Dylan!" yelled Colvin. "For fuck's sake, *what's happening?*"

"A Summoning. She's summoning a demon. It's coming here... now! Can't you smell it?"

"I can't smell anything." But he could. Impinging on the cloying odour of roses emanating from the sword, another sweet stench had begun to assail his nostrils, and a noise, like paper tearing, was coming from one end of the room, from the sliding doors, the glass of which had darkened as if heavily smoked. A mist was forming there, obscuring the whole wall.

"Simon! Cathy! Quickly, come here, into the centre of the room."

They ran to him, and he pulled them shoulder to shoulder, facing the growing, stinking fog. The ripping sound was increasing in volume, clashing horribly with and even threatening to drown out the sword's howling.

"Now listen to me," barked Dylan over the commotion. "You don't move from this spot, either of you, for anything! Do you understand me?"

They nodded, and he began to walk slowly around them. Their eyes followed him, and they both looked down as he completed his circuit; a scarlet ring had been left in his wake. It smouldered, it smoked, and then it erupted into small but dazzlingly bright, blue-white flames.

"This will help protect you. Don't, whatever you see, whatever you hear — *whatever happens* — move from this ring. Do so, and you are as good as dead."

"What about you?" shouted Colvin, barely able to hear himself above the deafening tumult. The question hung gaseous in the air, his breath in freezing plumes as the room's temperature plummeted.

"I have to leave." They looked disbelievingly at the angel, as if betrayed. "I have no choice. The thing that comes now and I cannot share the same space and time. It is not allowed. The repercussions would be terrible. I am here voluntarily. The demon has been summoned. It cannot leave, so I must. Do as I say. Protect yourselves. Protect each other, but don't leave the ring for *anything*! Good luck…"

… with which he disappeared, a pained expression on his face the last thing they saw. Pain because he had already stayed too long, or at leaving them to an uncertain fate, they would never know.

In spite of the peril they were in, Cathy bent to examine the circle of flames. They did not exude heat; neither did they burn the carpet. They neither grew nor diminished in size or brightness. She looked upwards, to comment on all this to Simon, when suddenly the sliding-door wall bellowed at them; the very fabric of the house gave voice to a cry of rage, and a dark spot in the centre of the writhing mist began to grow and open up to reveal… nothing. Beyond that hole was an eternity of featureless grey. Colvin knew what it was. He had been there once before.

The noise, little more than a random cacophony, began to form itself into garbled speech, which they could not make out until three words burst forth from the expanding fissure with such force they were almost pushed backwards out of their protective ring.

"BLOOD AND SOULS…"

They closed their eyes, shielded their ears, as this disembodied oath shook the room. When they looked again, the fog had begun to gather itself into a roughly human shape. It twisted and roiled; multihued tendrils spun out from it towards them, insubstantial but threatening coils which stopped just short of the flames and then retreated.

A wordless, frustrated roar arose from the misty figure, whose shape lost some of its consistency, as if it could only concentrate on one thing at a time. Finding unexpected resistance, needing to work out how to counter this, it had lost any grip on its semi-corporeal semblance, and fragmented.

The cloud blossomed backwards and outwards until it covered, like a translucent gauze, the whole of the sliding-door wall again, and there it solidified into an hideous, purulent film, from which came the reek of corrupted flesh.

Then the wall seemed to collapse backwards, across and beyond the roof terrace, into the night, away from the petrified couple, and became a vast, gaping maw from which a searing, fœtid saliva oozed. Teeth, huge, ragged and razor-sharp, began to form around this opening which sucked all the clean, icy air from the room and replaced it with foul gasses.

Colvin and Cathy were tossed in their tiny round sanctuary, nearly choking on this repulsive, billowing atmosphere as it was inhaled and exhaled about them. To avoid being dragged out, they fell to their knees and clung to each other. Nauseated, neither of them could resist staring at the horror before them.

The ragged teeth grew larger, surrounded now by slavering, malformed lips. Suddenly the whole mouth shot out towards them, attached to the wall's edges by a thin membrane against which it strained in its attempts to engulf them; to swallow them whole. Again, though, it was thwarted by the ring of fire; was unable to penetrate any space immediately above the flames. Inches from their faces, it snapped and snarled and spat, but nothing reached them. A tongue lolled out from the back of this dreadful throat, luminous pustules erupting across it as it tried to lap at them, to taste them, only to be beaten back time and time again by their supernatural protection.

The giant jaws withdrew at last, flowed and coagulated into the murky wall and then ceased to move at all, as if frozen.

This pause gave the couple a chance to catch their breaths, before the next attack. Neither of them spoke; could not have if they wanted to.

Then both clutched at their own heads, as their senses were assaulted by a barrage of colours that pervaded every part of them and threatened to drown them in an infinite, unihued wholeness. Colvin saw an endless blood red: he saw red, he smelled red, he heard red, he tasted red, he felt red; unable to escape its insidious, overwhelming attack upon his being.

Cathy saw, smelled, heard, tasted, felt waves of different colours, one after another, each threatening to suffocate her. Both of them retched violently, yet still saw nothing but these sentient, ravenous shades. It stopped, as suddenly as it began, and only then, in the ensuing lull, did they realise they were screaming.

Another hole opened in the fog-bound wall, and this one spiralled in front of them; more sounds poured from the mini-cyclone and formed themselves into words. The first thing Colvin heard was his children crying, *"Daddy! Daddy!"* He saw them through closed eyes, imploring him to help them; to save them from a danger he could not locate. He wept for them, called to them, as other voices joined theirs: *"Oh, Simon, please don't go! No! Please don't leave me!"* Elspeth! The mist was drawing out of him his darkest moments — his bleakest memories — was feeding on them and then spewing them back at him; pounding him with them. He tried to block the voices out by raising his own within his head. *Stop it! Stop it!* he thought; *please make it stop*, he begged; *I can't take it any more*, he whimpered; *just make it go away now...*

Cathy, too, was being mentally pulverised by traumatic sights and sounds from her past, from her childhood, as she sat sheltering in the cupboard under her parents' stairs while a massive thunderstorm tore around their house. She was alone, off from school with a fever, her parents at work, and the storm was all but overhead, crashing with force enough to rattle the windows, to shake the cupboard door she clung to in a desperate attempt to keep the thunder-monsters out. She was convinced they were out there, waiting for her. She knew they wanted her. She heard their dog running up and down the hallway, barking frantically, trying also to escape the growing turmoil; in its panic it knocked over a small bookcase, which fell across the doorway to the cupboard and locked the little girl therein for another six hours, screaming all the while to be let out and totally unheard until her father arrived home. The thunder had stopped hours before, but not the noises — not the monsters — she could hear them all afternoon, scratching to get in; to get her, to eat her alive.

Colvin, next to her but unable to help, was suddenly blown backwards by another ear-splitting yell from the wall ahead of them. He put out his good arm, to stop himself falling flat, and it landed outside of the ring of bright fire. In an instant, another foul-smelling tentacle writhed out towards him and grabbed his wrist. It burned. His mind exploded in a frenzy of red and black, as every dark thought, every unhealthy whim, every loathsome desire that he had ever experienced was dredged up and horrendously exaggerated to sickeningly unreal proportions. He saw his children again. They cried, and he laughed at them. He grabbed them; he threw them to the floor, and still he laughed in their terrified faces. He laughed as he hit them, as he bit them, as he hurt them. He laughed as he stripped them, as he tied them, as he whipped them. He laughed as he cut them, as he tore them, as he bled them. He laughed as he ripped them, as he fucked them, as he raped them. He laughed as he killed them, as he opened them, as he ate them. Even in death, dismembered, in bloody pieces before him, still they begged him to stop, told him they loved him, tugged and clawed at his arm…

… no, it was Cathy who pulled at his arm, and the vile images began to fade. Between them they dragged his hand back towards the flaming circle and as it touched this the tendril shrivelled up; a low, baffled-sounding whine escaped the wall. His hand bled from deep, raw gashes and blisters; he had vomited, without even realising it. He cried in her arms then, like a child, whilst their enemy, whatever it was, decided its next move against them.

A rattle of sinister, sibilant whispers blew around them on an unnatural breeze, as if a multitude of demonic conspirators debated how best to assault them. Cathy cradled Simon's head in her lap, brushed his hair back from a saturated brow, and wondered how much more he could take. She had no idea what he had encountered whilst out of their protective ring, and did not want to know. She knew only that he suffered. His eyes were wildly agitated, flicking from side to side in their sockets, still fearing attack from every corner. Then he seemed to go limp in her arms, and even slept briefly, fitfully, whilst their foe murmured and plotted around them.

His eyes were closed for no more than a minute or two, but when they reopened he appeared to have regained at least a tenuous grip on the sanity his lover feared had fled him for good. He croaked a word or two, and she bent her head down to hear him: "I love you," he sighed.

The demon or demons in the mist shrieked suddenly, as if offended or even wounded by the uttering of this endearment, though still there was no further barrage from the hell-wall.

Colvin spoke again, his voice a little stronger: "The sword."

"What about it?"

"Look at it."

Cathy turned and saw that it still glowed a brilliant, warm gold from the top of the bag it was in, across the other side of the room, as far from them in one direction as the sliding-door wall was in the other. Its howling had subdued now, to an insistent, almost crafty mewling. Its tone changed again slightly, seeming to acquire a sentient, more urgent edge, as if aware it was being discussed; as if trying to communicate with them.

"The fog avoids it," said Colvin, and this was so. Every inch of the room — floor, walls, ceiling — was spread across with spidery wisps of the wall's foggy ectoplasm, except for the areas immediately around the two of them, and around the sword.

Colvin looked hard into the eyes of Cathy then, and swallowed once, deeply, before saying, "I have to get it."

"*You can't!*" she cried. "Look what happened when your arm was grabbed. What chance would you stand out there on your own? You'd be driven mad, if not killed. I won't let you…"

"You can't stop me. Cathy, it's the only way."

"Then I'm coming with you…"

"That *is* crazy! Why risk both of us? We've only a got a little while, surely, before it attacks again. This is our one chance, and you've got to stay here. There's no point in both of us getting…"

He was interrupted by movement from the wall, as the mist leapt and heaved in anticipation of their plan, somehow aware that they were about to move against it. It pummelled them again with more disgusting mental images which they did their best to ignore, trying through gritted teeth to talk amidst this new onslaught.

"Then let me go instead," yelled Cathy. "You're already weakened by it. I'm stronger."

"But *I* know what to expect now. I think I can fight it off. I can…"

… with which he rolled out of her arms, across the floor and out of the ring of fire, all before she could react.

"*Simon!*" she screamed, but was powerless to help him as within a moment he was surrounded by liquescent strands that poured from the wall. They wrapped around him as he tried to stand and run towards the bag containing the sword. He was almost to it when the fog tripped him. Stumbling forward, his hand latched around the bag's handle and, as he was dragged back towards the hell-hole that formed itself once more into a ravenous, ragged-toothed orifice, he reached out with his injured arm for the very artefact which had inflicted that wound. His shout was not just one of pain, but of unbearable agonies of the spirit as sensations a hundred times more hideous and wicked than before invaded his mind and tried to tear it irreparably asunder.

His over-extended fingers found a purchase on the sword's hilt, and a sonorous, triumphant ululation tumbled from it as the weapon seemed to leap into his palm. Colvin felt a near-electric jolt through his arm, and a strength return with which he was able to counter, slightly, the evil thought projections which still bombarded him.

The mist seemed desperate to pull him into itself — to consume him — before he could acquire any more protective sustenance from the weapon, and Cathy could do nothing but look on, powerless to assist, as he was pulled right up to the opening. His legs splayed, and his feet pushed as best they could against the yielding substance in an attempt to avoid being dragged straight to Limbo (could any other fate result from such an absorption?).

He was pulled upright, and was on the verge of toppling forward into that endless, pitiless grey void when, with the last of his energies, he drew back his arm and threw the sword, broken point first, into its rapidly spiralling centre.

There was a wailing, far louder and more penetrating than anything which had preceded it, as the fog seemed to retreat and pour back into itself. Colvin was hurled upwards and outwards, across the length of the room where he landed in a tangled mess of flailing limbs which Cathy guessed could only be death throes, and then they were both being buffeted by a sucking gale of malodorous air as the demonic mist fled the room with a last, defeated gasp and left them, crumpled and motionless, in a sudden and deafening silence.

Cathy felt the seductive lure of consciousness, and her mind at first rejected its insistent beckoning, trying instead to opt for blissful unawareness. She knew she would awake to find her lover dead, and wanted rather to sleep forever, or to give herself up into oblivion's warm embrace and join him.

After a while, she knew she could do neither, and her eyes reluctantly fluttered open and fell upon the face of the room's large wall clock. It took her a while to realise why she could not read the time: the clock was no longer on the wall, but on the floor, upside down before her. The time finally began to register on her brain, which refused to accept the information offered it, deciding that the clock must have stopped. The relentless motion of its second hand belied this though, and she had to accept that just ten minutes had passed since Dylan had first encircled them in his ring of bright fire, which was now extinguished. She noticed, too, that the C.D. which Simon had put on still played in the background; had continued playing through all that had just happened.

Beyond the fallen clock, she could see Simon's body. She began to crawl painfully towards it, so that she could hold him, cradle him — his lifeless form — one last time. So sure was she that he was dead, when his hand moved a fraction of an inch, and he groaned, she let out a startled yelp and leapt up to run to him, smothering him with kisses and weeping over him, until he had to push her away a little, just to get some air.

She still held his head in her hands, framing his face, looking at him, desperately seeking some reassurance that he had survived his ordeal unscathed, but what she saw contradicted that hope. He stared vacantly before him, seeing her but not really registering who she was nor what had happened to them.

She kept repeating his name, over and over again, trying to see some spark of recognition, until she realised that he was trying to speak and so fell silent. She leaned forward to catch his words. There was only one: "'Phone."

"What do you…" she began, and then she heard it too. After everything they had been through, something as normal as the telephone ringing was bringing them both back to welcome sanity from the nightmare edges of a terror they had all too recently endured.

Without another word, Colvin stood, somewhat shakily, and left the room with a slow, weary, shuffling gait to answer the telephone on the landing. Cathy became dimly aware that, at ten past two in the morning, the call could not possibly be quite as normal as she had first hoped.

He returned. No time seemed to have elapsed. His face was still ashen, his voice still drained, devoid of emotion; devoid of anything. "It was Elspeth," he said, blankly. "The woman. She's taken the children."

REMINISCENCE (6)

S HE SITS, AND she waits. In her lap is a small black clutch-bag. Her
hands grip it tightly.

She opens her eyes briefly, shuts them again, and remembers.

She remembered the odious Mr. Frye. She had thought of him as that
for so long, she had forgotten his Christian name. Had she ever known
it?

He was, she supposed, her British equivalent to the American
agency she had used to hire those undesirables who carried out work
for her there. He boasted of connections with the British secret service,
via some possibly fictitious insurance company he claimed to be the
managing director of, which was apparently a front for all sorts of
nefarious goings-on.

She had always found it hard to believe that any government would
have had a use — in such a position of alleged authority — for a man
who seemed so permanently worried; for such a misfit. He was a tiny
man — almost *petit* — with a slightly hunched back and a peculiarly
sideways, near-crablike manner of walking. She had suspected that his
so-called network of agents was little more than an unsavoury collection
of the seedier type of ex-con.

His voice, half-wheeze, half-whine, had always grated on her, and
she avoided having to meet with him personally whenever possible.

Nevertheless, she liked to think that, had she been a witch of old, he would have been her familiar. Whilst most traditional witches and wizards had satisfied themselves with toads or rats for such mascots, so she had the odious Mr. Frye.

In any other circumstances, his perverse sexual appetites — with which she had ensnared him into her employ in the first place — would have made him a prime candidate for death by 'payment'. Instead, his value to her outweighed the repugnance he gave rise to — if only just — and she had put him to much well-paid use over the years.

His current service for her had been to kidnap the Colvin brats, an undertaking Frye was particularly well suited to. (She fully expected the demon to dispose of Colvin, and his woman, but had still decided to finish the job completely by eliminating his offspring too.)

Taking no chances, though, that Frye might slip up, she had chosen to possess him for the duration of the task. It was a hugely exhausting process, and drained her of what little strength remained after the fight at Tintagel.

Once secure in the knowledge that the demon had been dispatched to Colvin's home, she had not allowed herself the luxury of falling prey to the period of unconsciousness that usually followed such a Summoning; had fought instead to stay awake long enough to impose her will, at a distance, upon the odious Mr. Frye who, with his proximity to Colvin's brats, was just the man to grab them and take them to his warehouse which she knew to be nearby.

He had resisted, at first, her invasion of his mind, but was not strong enough wholly to repel her. So he had done her bidding.

✡   ✡   ✡

She opens her eyes briefly, shuts them again, and remembers.

She remembered sleeping then, a long, deep, untroubled sleep — rare, for her — and had awoken late the following afternoon. Her powers were still far from fully restored, but she had to see Frye, to ensure that all had gone according to plan, and also to devise a suitable way of extinguishing two tiny lives. (It seemed that, having taken her first innocent life at Tintagel, she was not beyond a couple more.)

It was then, just before setting off, that she divined her knowledge of Colvin's infuriating survival. What had she to do, to kill this man? Now she would have to keep his offspring alive, a perfect leverage, if ever there was one, in the next battle; and the next would have to be the last. She had begun to realise that she would only be able to recoup enough energy for one more round.

Frye, when she arrived at his offices, had been less than pleased to see her. "Madam, I take high exception at being used in such a manner, a mere puppet, and would respectfully request that you refrain from doing any such thing again."

His voice, as ever, had irritated her in an instant; his eyes, slightly shifty and anxious, twitched; his pale little face was podgy and grim. He sought solace, as he spoke, in the catamite upon his knee, whose naked back he stroked, uncaring of what she thought of his ever-lustful needs. This boy, no more than perhaps thirteen or fourteen years of age, picked at a loose-edged fingernail and stared with practised nonchalance into the middle distance, showing no interest whatsoever in his master's business.

She ignored Frye's affected indignation. "I need you to tell me exactly what happened."

"Madam, you were the one inside my fucking head. *You* tell *me* what happened!"

"Silence, little man! I had limited access, to your limited mind, and imbued you with certain powers. That is all. I have no clear memory of events during my occupation of you. Now, tell me."

His caressing of the youth grew more agitated. "I woke up. I got up. I went out," he began, determined to sound as furious at her treatment of him as he possibly could. "I arrived at some address I'd never been to before, and banged on the door. The nigger bitch who opened it demanded to know what I thought I was doing at such an ungodly hour. I was about to answer her — that I had absolutely no idea what the hell I was doing there either — when some incomprehensible garbage sprang from my lips instead and she fell to the floor. I went inside. I went upstairs. There were two half-'n'-half kids, asleep. I spoke some more mumbo-jumbo at them, too, and brought them downstairs to my car.

Now they're in the warehouse behind us, and they haven't woken up or moved once in all that time. I didn't hang around to see if the coon woman was dead or alive. There! End of story. Satisfied?"

"Quite, thank you. The children are to stay here until further notice."

"No fucking way!" He pushed the catamite from his lap, and the boy flew across the room to land, sulking petulantly, in a corner. "What am I supposed to do with a brace of half-chat sprogs running around the place?"

"They will not wake, until I so desire it. And *you* will do as you are told. It is what I pay you for. Now, take me to them."

Thoughts of the not insubstantial retainer she paid into his Swiss bank account each month induced in him a sudden air of compliant resignation, and he led her to the warehouse area of the building they were in, unlocking the doors and gesturing her forward, ahead of him, whilst he reached inside and fumbled for the light switches.

The flicker of overhead fluorescence steadied to reveal a large but virtually empty storage space. In the centre of this area, lying on wooden pallets with nothing but thin night-clothes to protect them from the unheated environment, were the boy and girl.

The woman heaved a deep, dissatisfied sigh. "Frye, you will get them beds and bedding. I do not wish them to die of exposure before I am ready for them. Do you understand?"

"Yes, madam." There was no longer any defiance in his weakling voice.

"For now, find something to put over them. Do you have anything, dust sheets or some such?"

"I'll attend to it."

She went over to where the children lay, in their sorcerous semi-coma, and Frye helped her to kneel beside them. She felt incredibly stiff, and ached far more than she had thought. Her period of recovery, before next attacking Colvin, would have to be substantial.

She looked at the children, and then strangely — certainly surprising herself — she stroked tenderly at their cold cheeks and held their hands in an almost affectionate manner. As if caught in an uncustomary moment of weakness, she stopped this as suddenly as it had begun.

"Help me up, Frye," she snapped, and he did so.

Back in the office area, at the front of the warehouse, she repeated her instructions regarding arrangements to be made for the children, and had him promise that all would be done before the end of the day.

"I will return in a few days' time, Mr. Frye, probably early next week. I expect them to be alive and well. They will not require sustenance; at least not yet. And you are not to touch them, do you understand? Either of them. Do I make myself quite clear?"

He was under no illusion as to what she implied, and bitterly resented the insinuation. Rancour rekindled, he snarled his answer: "Quite clear, thank you, *madam*." The title was used without respect — was all insult — but such pettiness was meaningless to her. She was certain that her orders would be obeyed to the letter. Frye knew a little, though not all, about the powers she could wield, and he was not about to defy her.

Their meeting was over.

✡ ✡ ✡

She opens her eyes briefly, shuts them again, and remembers.

She remembered returning to her apartments and preparing for her long-overdue period of recovery. She would put herself into a trance, not unlike the one affecting the Colvin brats, which would last for an unknown number of days, during which her mental and physical energies would restore themselves as best they could. Once fully recovered, she would awake, and be ready for the next, the final round in her battle against Simon Colvin, which if she won would result in another restoration; that of her soul. Then, only then, could she die.

As she had begun, in the warmth of her bed, to chant the necessary incantations required to induce several days of complete unconsciousness, a small part of her mind had wandered off in a most unlikely direction, to a memory from her childhood, so very many years before.

She remembered a trip she had made, with her parents, to Stonehenge. In those days, the site had not yet become a tourist attraction, but simply sat on Salisbury Plain, awaiting discovery by anyone and everyone, there to be meandered through at will, which she recalled doing with an incredible sense of awe at the sheer scale of those great stones towering above her. She remembered peering up from the bases of the tallest sarsens, watching the clouds scud by and give rise to the illusion that it was the stones themselves that were moving, threatening to topple over onto her. This did not scare her at all, and she had simply darted from one to another, laughing and looking upward all the while.

That was during happier times, of which there had been very few, even in her childhood. Her father had been particularly ebullient that day, having recently sold some of his artwork, and he was sober. She recalled being lain by him across what would later be known as the 'altar stone' — merely, in fact, a fallen sarsen — while he had sketched her, and his wife looked on, smiling for once, her face unusually blemish-free. It would be a few more months before her mother died at the hands of her drunken husband, beaten to a bloody pulp whilst their eight-year-old daughter looked on in horror.

Several times since then, in the course of her long, long adulthood, she had returned to Stonehenge, and each time the prehistoric circle seemed to have shrunk further and further from those first impressions, when as a child she had run carefree amongst the monoliths and begged to be allowed to stay there forever.

She had not thought of that moment for many years, and knew not why she did so then; but as this and all other senses slipped from her, and a curtain of blackness fell across her exhausted mind, a plan had begun to form.

✳   ✳   ✳

All this she remembers.

Still she sits. Still she waits…

BOOK FOUR (An End)

You know that I care what happens to you,
And I know that you care for me too,
So I don't feel alone,
Or the weight of the stone,
Now that I've found somewhere safe
To bury my bone
And any fool knows a dog needs a home,
A shelter from pigs on the wing

Roger Waters
Pigs On The Wing

CHAPTER THIRTEEN

(Yet Another, Further, Different Monday)

"WHERE ON EARTH do you think you've been?" shouted Simon Colvin, at Dylan the angel, who stood on his and Cathy Beauchamp's doorstep. "It's been five days! Where the fuck were you when we needed you?"

"Simon, I…"

"Five days!"

"Simon, I…"

"Do you know where they are? Is that why you're here? Tell me!"

"Simon!"

"Yes, what?" He glowered.

"May I come in?"

"Yes —" this from Cathy, at the foot of the stairs — "Dylan, do please come in."

Colvin moved begrudgingly aside to let the angel pass into the house, then closed the door, turned and followed them up to the living room.

Once there, Colvin stood stormily by the sliding doors, scene of so much recent horror, as the others sat. Dylan apologised for his absence — fidgeting all the while with a patched leather shoulder bag resting on his lap — although "I've been otherwise engaged" was all he would say in his defence.

"Otherwise engaged!" This set Colvin off again. "My children are missing, and you're *otherwise engaged*! Doing what, may I ask?"

"I cannot tell you." It was unlike the angel to be so blunt in his refusal to reveal information. He was usually far more genially circumspect. It was obvious, also, that he was uncomfortable with this new, directly assertive rôle.

"Can't or won't?" Colvin was relentless — cared nothing, this time, for Dylan's distress — was only interested in discovering what the angel did or didn't know about his children's whereabouts.

"Both, really," offered Dylan, not a response likely to assuage the other's anger. "I *have* been engaged in tracking down the woman and your children, *but* —" he added quickly, as Colvin was about to ask for details — "with little success, I'm afraid."

"So what *do* you know?"

"Well, most importantly, we know that the children are alive."

Colvin thought he was going to faint, such was the wave of inexpressible relief that washed over him then, and Cathy came over to hug him, an echo of a similar, less intimate gesture some months before. He walked with her across the room, sat next to her on the sofa and looked at Dylan, wanting to apologise for his aggression, but he saw in those beautiful angelic eyes a sense that all was not being revealed. "I feel another 'but' coming on…" he said.

"The children are alive, Simon — we would know if they had come to any harm — any… lasting harm — *but*… they are under the control of the woman. She must have them in some form of glamour, a trance, if you will, which we cannot penetrate. Nor can we locate them, so intense is its influence."

"What of the woman? You must know where she is?"

The angel's discomfiture visibly increased, and he squirmed a little in his armchair. "She, too, must have been in a near-comatose state, to avoid detection."

"But you know where she lives, right? We can go there and beat it out of her!"

"Simon, I… we — um — no…" This was painful to behold, and as obviously pained the angel, being so evasive. "It's just a pity we no longer have the sword…"

"But we do!" exclaimed Cathy. "It's still here."

"Here…?"

"Yes, we found it on the floor after… after the other night. Look."
She took a tea towel from the low table between them, and reached
behind the sofa to retrieve and bring forth the sword. "Simon's still the
only one who can touch it unharmed. Do you know why?"

"I think so, yes, but why is it still here? How did it remain?"

"It was just lying on the floor, by the doors, after the demon fled. And
look, Dylan, at its point." She offered the weapon forward, but the angel
declined to touch it, noticing instead that it was once more sharpened to
a razor's-edge and daggerlike point. It was still slightly shortened, to the
length it had become after the end had snapped off, but was otherwise
in all respects a fully functioning sword. In proximity to Dylan, it began
to buzz and to glow in a subdued, unthreatening way, and the scent of
roses was again evident.

"Did you do that, sharpen it?"

"No," said Colvin, "that's how we found it."

"Curious…"

"Curiouser and curiouser," mumbled Cathy, mainly to herself but
making Dylan glance up in puzzlement at her deliberate misuse of the
language. "I mean," she went on, "of all the fantasy-fiction clichés, I
just can't believe that we've actually found ourselves in possession of
a magical sword! Couldn't we use something a little less… generic?"
She looked at the others' blank expressions and apologised for her less
than appropriate flippancy. "It's a writer thing," she added, by way of
defence.

"I only wish," continued the angel, "that I'd thought to leave you
with it, in my protective circle, for use against the demon. I should have,
but in my hurry to leave…"

"Yes," interrupted Colvin, "why was that? You said something about
you and the demon not being able to share the same time and space.
What was that all about?"

"Well, it's…"

"… yes, I know, it's kind of hard to explain. Isn't everything? Look,
just tell us."

Dylan smiled, and relaxed a little, while still seeming somewhat ill
at ease. "Do you understand, both of you, the concept of matter and
anti-matter?" They nodded, although Cathy said she thought the latter

was merely a theoretical possibility. "Oh, no, it exists, all right, though rarely on any earthly plane of existence. Anyway, if you're aware of the cataclysmic effects of matter coming into contact with anti-matter — the disastrous results that would ensue — then imagine, if you will, a similar concept of (for the want of something better to call them) evil and anti-evil. For a demon and I to come into contact with each other would cause irreparable damage to the structure of all existence, on every plane. I can't explain how, exactly, but it would be so, and it's why I had to leave in such a rush. I'm just sorry you went through so much, because I didn't think. If you hadn't needed to leave the ring to get the sword…" He trailed the sentence off, unfinished, seeing Colvin's face reliving memories of their experience against the demon. "Well, I have to be going."

"Going. Where?" asked Colvin, sensing a sudden desperation in the angel to be away from there; to be somewhere else. "Do you have an idea where the kids are? Or the woman?" He could not believe how easily he had been led away from the matter at hand, that of finding and saving his children. All his earlier aggression towards the angel arose again, so convinced was he that something was still being kept from him. "What aren't you telling me?"

"Simon… I… I'm sorry — um — please… trust me." His eyes seemed to implore them to believe him, and Cathy put a hand on Colvin's arm.

"I think we should, Simon, don't you? Dylan wouldn't let us down, would you, Dylan?"

The angel, though, failed to make eye-contact with either of them, and simply stood with another mumbled apology, heading for the stairs.

"Where's your Walkman?" Colvin had been searching their bedroom since Dylan's over-hasty and embarrassed departure.

"In the wardrobe," said Cathy. "Why?"

"I'm following him. He's up to something. I need noise to block out my thoughts. He mustn't know I'm there."

"What! How do you know he won't know? And what makes you so sure he's up to something? He just seemed sorry, to me, that he'd not left us with the sword."

"You don't know him as well as I do. He's never been as… uncertain…

as that before. I *know* something's wrong, and I'm going to find out what it is. And I've no idea if I *can* avoid his knowing I'm following him, but I've got to try." He had found the small personal stereo and was now rummaging through a pile of cassette tapes, looking for something suitably raucous to play at maximum volume, hoping to blot out anything that might alert the angel to his presence. "This'll do."

So, with AC/DC's *If You Want Blood, You've Got It* distortedly blaring into his ears and threatening to render him all but insensible, he set off on foot in search of Dylan, glad of the angel's resolution these days to walk more often than vanish.

Lucking out on the direction he took, he soon spotted Dylan a block or two ahead on the King's Road, striding over the brow of a railway bridge, heading east. The angel showed no sign of suspecting he was being followed. Even when Colvin nearly lost sight of him, passing through crowds crossing Sloane Square, it did not seem a deliberate attempt at concealment.

There were fewer places for Colvin to hide himself, less camouflaging bustle, once they entered Cliveden Place, and he had to resort to a more stereotypically clandestine dash from tree to tree, behind which he tucked himself whilst watching Dylan's progress. There had been a brief moment of panic, while the music stopped and the tape needed turning over, when he feared discovery, but the angel had seemed too intent on locating his destination.

Towards the end of Eaton Gate, Dylan turned left into Eaton Square, along the terraces of huge Georgian houses. He seemed to be seeking a specific address. When he stopped outside one in particular, looking up at its imposing façade, Colvin was about twenty yards from him, crouched down behind a parked car.

Eventually, and after checking the contents of his shoulder bag — it struck Colvin, then, that he had never seen the angel carrying anything before — Dylan mounted the stone steps up to the house's large, black-painted entrance door and pressed at a small brass bell-push.

It took a very long time for the door to be opened, during which Colvin crept closer to the house, eventually stopping behind a nearby stone column from where he could hear the scraping of bolts and locks, having chanced silencing his musical camouflage.

Then voices; a woman's first: "What do *you* want?"

Dylan's: "I offer you no harm."

"Of course you do." Colvin recognised this voice, now. It was the woman, his adversary, but he was shocked into inactivity; too stunned to move.

"Trust me," said Dylan. Colvin could not believe the depth of the angel's betrayal.

"Why should I?"

"Because I can help you. You still have the sword-point?"

"What if I have?" She was wary.

"Do you have it?"

"Yes."

"Then there is a use for it, one I can help you put it to."

"Why are you telling me this?"

"Let me come in, and I will explain."

Colvin heard the door close, and only then allowed himself to breathe. His legs lost all their strength, and he slid his back down the column to sit shaking on the pavement. As his thoughts began to refocus, his first reaction was to run up the steps and demand entrance, insist upon knowing what was going on, get his children back. Then he considered the alternatives. What chance would he have on his own, against two supernaturally powerful enemies? None. Instead, he moved to one side of the pillar and down another set of steps to a small basement yard. There he concealed himself behind a large, unruly wisteria, which grew up from a wooden trough and clung both to the building and to the front railings above him. From here he could see without being seen, and awaited Dylan's reappearance.

After a quarter of an hour, he heard the door's latch again, and the angel came out, turning to speak to the woman whom Colvin still could not see. "You understand, now, what is expected of you, if events take that particular turn?"

"I do."

"Then I have something to give you." Colvin saw Dylan delve into his shoulder bag, and produce from it a small revolver. He proffered the pistol, and then a larger, oilcloth-wrapped package towards the doorway; and far older, wizened hands reached out to take them both.

Without another word, the angel turned, walked down the steps and away from the house, back in the direction of Sloane Square.

It was several minutes before Colvin could even move. He was deeply baffled by Dylan's actions, and more hurt by them than he would ever have thought possible. Why had he been through all this; why had the angel helped him so often, only to sell him out at the last moment? What of the children? Where were they? *How* were they? Only Dylan would know — lying, cheating Dylan — and Colvin had to find out, one way or another.

Eventually, careless of the lack of music, he went up the basement steps to the street and set off in pursuit of the treacherous angel.

CHAPTER FOURTEEN (A Familiar Death)

SIMON COLVIN GOT as far as Sloane Square without having caught up with Dylan, and began to wonder if the angel had not simply disappeared. Seeing a taxi with its FOR HIRE light on, he flagged it down and went straight home, his mind still in turmoil from all he had learned.

He told Cathy what had gone on, and she was as dumbstruck as he by Dylan's actions.

"*Why* would he do that, Simon? It doesn't make any sense. What are we going to do now?"

"Well, I'm going right back there now, to Eaton Square, to the woman's, and finding out where the kids are."

"I'll come..." she began, but was interrupted by a knock at the door. She went downstairs and then reappeared with Dylan in tow. Her eyes begged Simon to remain calm, conveyed that she had not revealed what they knew.

"Dylan," said Colvin, "hi!" He hoped this did not come across as falsely as it sounded to his own ears; hoped his welcoming smile was more grin than grimace.

"Hello, Simon. Sorry to have dashed off like that and left you here. I needed to go for a bit of a walk. To clear my head a little."

"So you didn't meet anyone while you were out?"

"Um... no... yes, I mean, why do you ask?"

Colvin lost it then, big time, and flew across the room, grabbing Dylan by the collar and forcing him hard against the wall. Prints shook with the vibration, and one fell to the floor with a splintering of glass. "Because I *know* where the fuck you went! Now what are you playing at?"

"Where I went?" The angel was taken aback, but showed little if any fear.

"You know what I mean, you bastard! The woman's. What were you doing there? And I want the truth!"

"I… I cannot tell you, Simon."

"And why not?"

"The rules…"

"*Look, fuck you, Dylan, and fuck your goddamned rules!*" He punctuated every syllable with another shake of the angel's collar, another heavy impact against the wall. Cathy pulled at his arm, yelled at him to back off. Eventually he let go, with a final thump, and began to pace the floor in front of Dylan, who asked to be allowed to explain.

"More lies?"

"No, Simon. Just as much truth as I'm able to reveal."

"Please, darling," said Cathy, "let him speak."

Colvin's furious silence was all the assent they were going to get, and so Cathy asked the angel to sit and account for his actions.

"Thank you. Well, yes, as you obviously now know, I did go to see the woman, but you have to believe me when I tell you it had absolutely no bearing on your involvement with her. I…"

"*No bearing?*" Colvin still fumed; still paced. "You told me you didn't know where she was!"

"No I didn't, Simon. I told you only that she had *been* in a near-comatose state, not that she still was, or that we knew not where to find her."

"Look, it's smart-arsed answers like that are going to get you another beating…"

"*Simon —*" this from Cathy, who insisted that Colvin sit down, which reluctantly he did — "Go on, please, Dylan. You were saying?"

"I was saying that my meeting had no bearing on Simon and…"

"But what about the children?" Colvin could not contain himself.

"You had her there, and did nothing to get them back! Were they there? Did you even see them?"

"No, they were not there. But I had her assurance that they are safe and well."

"*Where* are they?"

"Please, Simon, let me come to that. Let me tell you what I need to tell you first, in the way I need to tell it."

A warning glance from Cathy subdued Colvin's impulse to push for more, and he simply sat back, arms crossed, determined to ride out the angel's story, if he could, without another word.

"The reason we could not find the woman is because, as we suspected, she was in a trance of sorts, one which has restored and even increased her energies. She only awoke from this state earlier today, and I must warn you, Simon, she is now incredibly strong, physically as well as mentally. It's as if she has been storing up all this power somehow, waiting for what must surely be your final encounter.

"As a result of the meeting, I have some idea of the form this last battle will take — where and when — and, I think, what part your children will play in it."

He now had the undivided attention of them both, and Colvin especially showed remarkable restraint in not speaking up — asking for more — realising, perhaps, that silence would actually bring the answers he sought all the quicker.

Dylan continued: "It is to take place at Stonehenge, tomorrow night…"

"*Stonehenge!*" It was Cathy's turn to interrupt, for which she apologised, but still had to know. "So that place really does have some mystical significance?"

"To be honest, Cathy, no, I don't believe it does. I think it just appeals to the woman's sense of the grandiose, her setting this encounter there. It may have some meaning for *her* as a venue, other than its obvious seclusion, but I'm certainly not aware of any supernatural connotation. That doesn't mean there isn't one, of course…"

"Can we get back to the point," insisted Colvin.

"Sorry, Simon. Yes, well, you are to meet her there tomorrow night, at midnight, alone. It is my guess that she will want to trade the sword for your children."

"Oh, shit."

"Indeed."

"What am I supposed to do?"

"That, Simon, only you can decide. You know what it means if the woman gets the sword. We all know what the children mean to you. I cannot make that decision for you. Nobody can."

"Cathy?"

His lover just looked at him, and shrugged. It was not a dismissive gesture. She had opinions, that much was obvious, but was not going to voice any of them, at least not yet.

"Oh, shit, shit, shit…" repeated Colvin. "Okay, so the children are unharmed, you're sure of that?"

"Yes. What point would there be in the woman hurting them? She needs you to need them; has to have them there for you *to* need."

"Then unless we can come up with anything else in the meantime, I guess all we can do is go there and… wing it. Try to get the kids *and* keep the sword. But I warn you, Dylan, if it comes down to it — down to one or the other — I'll let the sword go."

The angel nodded.

"Wait…" Another thought came to Colvin's mind. "What about the sword-point she has, and the gun you gave her? What have they to do with all this?"

"As I told you before, the rest of my meeting, including those artefacts, had nothing to do with you. You are going to have to trust me on this."

"And why the fuck should I?"

"Look, the reason I left here before, so abruptly, is that I can't lie to you, Simon. An angel cannot lie. You were asking too many questions, and I was having difficulty evading them. You weren't supposed to know of the meeting at all. I don't even know how you did."

Colvin liked having something, for once, over on Dylan. "That's for me to know…" was all he said, with a deliberate air of mystery. "All right, let's say for the moment that I'll trust you, though I don't see why I should. What about the children? You must know where they are too, by now. You can't have gone there, spoken to her, and not found that much out."

"Simon, I… I can't tell you what else we discussed…"

"Do you know where they are?"

"Yes. Yes, I do."

"Then why don't we go and get them now, before tomorrow night?"

"I cannot tell you where they are. I am not allowed to. It would be interfering; against the… *conditions*…"

Exasperated, Colvin bristled. "Rules, conditions, call them what you will. You tell me where my children are, and you tell me right now, or I don't go anywhere tomorrow night. I don't do another damned thing for you!"

"But you *have* to go." The angel seemed aghast, as if defiance on Colvin's part had never been considered.

"Try me."

"Simon, I *can't* tell you. Look, you can be made to go, you know."

"Is that a threat?" This was a genuine, rather than a merely rhetorical question. Such things as the use of force being so alien to Dylan, his meaning had been far from explicit.

"You are the only one who can fight this fight for us, Simon. You know that. But you are not needed to do so willingly. It's best, of course, but you can be… *impelled*."

"Oh, I'm sure I can." For some reason, Colvin did not feel perturbed by this knowledge. Instead it seemed only to confirm many previously uncertain assumptions. "Okay, let's try this for size. You tell me where my children are, or I top myself, here and now, and you've got no-one left to do your dirty work for you."

"Top yourself?" The angel did not recognise the phrase.

"Kill myself. Here. Now. So tell me!"

"You wouldn't."

"I would, and I will, if you don't tell me where to find the kids." He bent and picked up the magical sword, placing the blade against his bared wrist. "I'll do it!"

"*Simon!*" Cathy hissed, shocked at this rapid turn of events. "*Don't…*"

"Doesn't it occur to any of you, if my children die, my life's not worth living anyway. I love them. They *are* my life. I left their mother, not them, even if it meant doing both."

The sword, though, had other ideas. It bucked in Colvin's hand, refused to rest in place upon his arm. An alarmed, resistant wailing emanated from it.

"That sword cannot take your life," said Dylan, quietly. "It's likely that it wouldn't be able to aid anyone in taking their own life."

"That's as may be, but I've got plenty of other things here that'll do the job. Knives in the kitchen and…"

"Okay, Simon. You've made your point. If I tell you where your children are, will you promise me that you won't try to rescue them?"

"Oh, *talk sense*! What am I supposed to do, send them a fucking postcard!"

"Listen to me. They, too, are in a trancelike state. If you tried to wake them from it, or to move them, it might kill them. It would be…"

"It '*might*'?"

"Yes, it might kill them, Simon."

"That's a chance I'm willing to take."

"What about your wife? What about Elspeth?"

"She doesn't know what's going on. She doesn't need to know about this, either. She's been dealing with the police and so on, treating the whole thing as a kidnapping, which is what she believes it is. What else *can* she do? I could hardly tell her the truth. She's been going crazy, though, 'phoning here nearly every hour, blaming me, wanting to know what I'm doing to help. I'm even booked to do a T.V. appeal with her in a couple of days."

"So what *does* she know about what's happened?"

"She remembers answering the door to someone on the night the kids were taken, but she can't even recall if they were male or female. She remembers a man, but then a woman's voice; thinks perhaps there were two of them. The next thing she knew was coming to, on the floor, and the kids gone."

"And you would put your children, her children too, at risk with this foolhardy rescue plan of yours?"

"Yes."

Dylan was silent for some time, before saying resignedly, "Then I guess I had better tell you where they are, hadn't I?"

"I think you'd better."

"This is wholly against the rules, you know, Simon. There could be repercussions."

"Screw the repercussions! I want my children back. Tell me!"

The angel sighed. "They are being kept at a warehouse in a place called Carshalton. Do you know where that is?"

"It's not too far from here, maybe half an hour or so's drive."

"Well, that is where they are. I know the address, and can take you there, if you're *really* sure you want to go. I think I should come as well, don't you? I may be able to help."

"That would be a first," said Colvin bitterly.

This particular car journey was undertaken in an atmosphere totally different to the last. There was almost no conversation, apart from Dylan's revealing of their destination's full address, and Cathy's navigating via the *A-Z* as they neared it.

There was no game plan. Colvin had no idea of what he would find at the warehouse, nor of what he would do when they arrived. The urge to get there — to see and hopefully to save his children — overrode all.

The warehouse turned out to be on a small industrial estate, half a dozen identically sized units on a nondescript plot. They pulled up, at first, before the gates to the estate, debating the best course of action. Deciding there was none, it was agreed instead to brazen things out and simply march straight on in there.

Parking outside the unit Dylan had told them of — which bore the legend 'International Insurance Ltd.' (*an odd venture to run from a warehouse*, thought Colvin) — they noticed one other car, a battered old Bentley, in the allocated spaces.

Now they were there, none of them seemed ready to be the first to move, though each for a very different reason. The angel feared what might happen, as a result of this rash action on Simon's part. Colvin himself feared what he might find when he got inside. Cathy feared that she was losing touch with any real involvement in events;

that she was no longer a part of what was happening, no more than a bystander.

With a suddenness which made the other two jump, Colvin reached for the car's door handle and was up and out of the vehicle in one swift movement, heading at a pace for the warehouse's glass-fronted entrance.

Soon the three of them stood in a relatively plush and unoccupied reception area. Closer examination, while they weighed up what to do having encountered no-one upon entering, revealed the area's lavishness to be somewhat superficial, as was that of the office they moved on into.

From there, into a dingy corridor, which is where Dylan found the bloodstains.

There was a small patch, semi-congealed, in which thicker, darker matter could be seen, on a wall near double doors to the warehouse proper. A trail led from this, down the wall and onto the floor where a larger pool was found, and from which a further ribbon of blood led under the doors and into the storage area.

None of them spoke. Colvin's breathing had quickened to an alarming rate, and he felt his already slender grip on things sliding away to be replaced with gruesome images of what they might find on the other side of those doors.

The doors themselves were slightly ajar, the lock having been smashed apart, although it was impossible to see through the tiny crack between. Dylan made a move towards them, but was beaten there by Cathy, who barred his way. She looked at Simon, who spoke in a harsh whisper.

"I can't go in there, Cathy. I can't see them, if they're… you know…"

"I'll do it. You two wait here."

"Do you want me to come?" asked Dylan.

"No."

She pushed her way through. It was very dark inside. She chose not to leave the doors wide open, but closed them together again behind her, opting to grope around for light switches which she knew must be just to one side or other of the doorframe.

There was a silence, which seemed to those left outside to last an age.

Then they heard Cathy's voice.

"Oh, Jesus fucking Christ! Oh, God, no!"

This was too much — worse than any reality — and Colvin leapt for the doors, followed just behind by the angel.

Cathy stood a few feet away, her back to them. Beyond her could be seen two tiny human forms, lying close together on the floor between Cathy and two empty camp-beds.

Colvin rushed to his lover's side, and looked at the bodies.

Both were horribly, humiliatingly mutilated, but he recognised neither. Of the children, there was no sign.

Reminiscence (7)

S HE SITS, AND she waits. In her lap is a small black clutch-bag. Her
hands grip it tightly.

She opens her eyes briefly, shuts them again, and remembers.

She remembered waking from her long, restorative, unnatural sleep,
feeling incredibly groggy but otherwise fine, better than she had for
many months — *years?*

She got up from her bed, bathed and then dressed, all before going to
her front door to examine the pile of newspapers on the coir matting,
discovering that she had been unconscious for five days.

It was instinct rather than appetence which then made her feel
ravenously hungry, and she went to the kitchen to prepare and consume
a huge breakfast.

She felt not just well, not just refreshed, but amazingly fit and strong;
ready for anything. Anything, that is, except for the ringing of the
doorbell and the appearance at her apartments of the angel.

Their exchange had not taken long. She had learned things of great
importance to her, but had had to trade for them with information of
her own, such as the whereabouts of the Colvin brats.

Realising that she would have to move them, earlier than planned,
she had set off in the direction of the odious Mr. Frye's warehouse.

The taxi journey from London to Carshalton was spent going over the whole scheme in her head. After all these years, she knew that nothing, no matter how seemingly arbitrary, happened without a reason, and even her very last thoughts as she had slipped into her long period of rest — those of Stonehenge — had gelled while she slept into a complete plan of action.

It now suited her purpose that the — *what did Frye call them?* — 'sprogs' still lived, even if she was going to have to wake them before she had originally intended.

Their use to her, in the final conflict with their father, was invaluable. The venue, too, was perfect. It had to be there, she knew. If asked, though, she could not have explained why.

The taxi arrived at the industrial estate, and she asked the driver to wait. A little over an hour had elapsed since her meeting with the angel, and she hoped to be way ahead of Colvin if he, as she fully expected, was heading this way as well.

Walking from the gates through the car park, she noticed that Frye's beaten-up old Bentley was outside the warehouse unit. That was unusual; he rarely spent any more weekday time at his offices than he absolutely had to.

Entering the building, the reception area was devoid of activity. There was usually a young woman at the desk, whose job it was to dissuade any potential customers from trying to arrange insurance there; from discovering there were no actual facilities for doing so.

Thinking back, though, the receptionist had not been present the last time she had been there either; the day after the brats were brought there. Perhaps Frye did not want (comparatively) innocent witnesses around, when such things as kidnapping and hostage-holding were afoot at the premises.

She moved through the entrance area into Frye's office, which was empty also, and from there into the corridor leading to the warehouse itself.

Here, at the end of the long, poorly lit passageway, she found the boy, Frye's catamite, standing to attention at the doors to the storage area.

He watched her approach, yawning in a manner both insolent and bored in equal measures. She could imagine him practising such looks for hour upon hour in a mirror somewhere, acting out his rôle whilst applying the make-up his master demanded of the succession of similarly vulnerable, malleable youngsters that had kept him company over the years.

She had no time to waste on this urchin. "Frye?" was all she said.

"Not here," drawled the boy.

"Let me through." It was a demand. The matter was not open for debate.

"Can't." He raised a hand before his face, palm outwards, fingers upwards, and examined his nails intently, believing the exchange to be over.

The speed with which she grabbed his throat — the ease with which she lifted him clear of the floor — surprised even her. The youth, however, had expected no such thing. One brief, hoarse gasp was the only sound he made as she squeezed all the harder. His eyeballs bulged. His tongue lolled. Urine seeped across the cloth of his trousers. Then she drew back her arm, child in hand, and smashed his head against the bare breeze-block wall. It made contact with a sickening, squelching thud, a loud snapping of neckbones, and as she let go he seemed to hang there, suspended for a second or two, before sliding down into a crumpled heap on the cold concrete floor. The back of his head, a mash of brain, bone, skin and hair, gaped open at her feet, and blood poured from this gory cavity towards her shoes; she had to back away from him rapidly to avoid being splashed.

Moving to one side, she tested the doors to the warehouse and found them locked. One push against the point at which they met shattered the lock and they flew apart. She bent to grab one ankle of the dead boy, dragging him after her into the storage area. Three people were therein. Two were unable to know of her entrance; they were unconscious. The third was too engrossed in what he was doing to have been aware of anything else.

Frye was kneeling at the camp-bed containing Colvin's four-year-old son. His head was bent over the boy's hips, and was moving rapidly, as was his hand between his own legs.

The woman brought the catamite's body over until she stood just behind Frye's hunched form. She dropped the youth's leg noisily to

187

the floor, but still the man continued. So she bent her own head, a mere inch from his, and whispered into his ear, "Mr. Frye."

His head shot up, and would have collided with hers had she not pulled back in time.

The tiny man twisted around and tried to stand then, all in one clumsy movement, stumbling as he did so and falling at her feet. His hands landed in the growing pool of blood still oozing from the corpse there, and he slipped flat, face downward in the sticky fluid. The woman raised her foot and placed it upon his neck, pinning him down while she looked around the warehouse.

First, she took hold of the covers that were drawn back to the foot of the camp-bed, and pulled them up to re-cover the boy. Looking across at the other cot, she saw that the girl's covers, too, were lowered; the night-dress raised.

Dragging Frye to his feet, she put her face in front of his. Her eyes turned from their customary bluish-purple to a near-red, as she snarled, *"Did you touch her?"*

"No!" he shrieked, choking and spitting another's blood from his mouth as he stuttered. "I was just… just looking…"

"She's not tampered with?"

"No. No, I promise you, no. Please, I didn't mean it. It was only the boy. I've this weakness, you see. I'm so weak. Oh, please, madam. Please don't hurt me. Please don't…"

She pushed him roughly away from her, and he stood quivering, pathetic, tears coursing down his podgy cheeks and mingling with the blood already on them.

She looked at him from head to toe, disgust plainly drawn across her features, and saw that his so-called manhood hung limply out of his trousers, between his legs. He did not move as she approached him; did not even flinch as she reached out her hand to grab him there.

In one swift movement, she squeezed, she twisted, she yanked. There was a sound of tearing flesh, and a last loud popping of rent sinew, then her hand came free, full of his dismembered genitalia; blood gushed from the wound and sprayed across the floor.

His scream started deep down in the pit of his stomach, and was as low in tone, but by the time it exited his wide-open mouth it had risen in pitch to a piercing screech no man — no human, even — should ever have been capable of venting. He stood stock-still, not daring to look down at what she had done to him, knowing full well from the dampness spreading outwards that he was no longer whole. Then he simply toppled over, and lay next to the body of his catamite, shocked into immobility. Here, he knew, he would bleed to death.

The last thing he saw, as consciousness began to flee him, was the woman leaning forward, and he felt her press something from her hand into his open mouth. He had no strength left to resist, and there it stayed, halfway down his throat as gradually he died.

Rapidly, she moved around this scene and picked up the children, one at a time, carrying their all but lifeless forms out of the warehouse, away from the carnage and into the reception area where she laid them down on the couches there.

She returned one last time to the storage area, and upon leaving pulled the double doors to as best she could. That was the last she ever saw of the odious Mr. Frye.

✠   ✠   ✠

She opens her eyes briefly, shuts them again, and remembers.

She remembered leaving the warehouse and returning to her apartments with the children. Again, she would have to be quick with all she needed to do, in order to leave before Colvin came calling there too, as no doubt he would.

She had awoken the children as easily as she had (through Frye) entranced them. Their suggestible minds were open to acceptance of anything she sowed in them, and they readily consented to come with her. She was a friend of their father, whom they would see tomorrow, she told them, and they believed.

When they had arrived at her home, she led the children to a separate basement flat where much of her occult apparatus and arcana was stored.

"Would you like to help me play a game?" she asked them, and they gleefully agreed, assisting her with lighting a burner over which she placed and heated a cast-iron smelting crucible. Into this she dropped a small piece of shiny metal, and together they watched it melt and bubble above the fierce flames. The boy, Sam, was allowed to say when all of the crucible's contents were molten, but only the girl, Sarah, was permitted to carry, in protective mitts, the substance over to a set of iron moulds which the woman had unwrapped from an oilcloth whilst all this went on, and into which the liquid metal was poured and allowed to cool.

After all this activity, the children not surprisingly claimed hunger (having not eaten for five days), and so the woman fed them hurriedly, keen to be away again as soon as possible.

"We are going on a little trip," she told them, "to see some stones. Some very large, very old stones."

As with their outing to 'a castle that isn't there anymore', the children were less than inspired by this prospect, but dutifully went along with their daddy's friend in another taxi to Waterloo Station, and thence onto a train bound for Salisbury; bound for Stonehenge; bound for Armageddon.

✳   ✳   ✳

She opens her eyes briefly, shuts them again, and recalls all that she has remembered.

She had remembered the Devil, her evening with Him, so many long years ago.

She had remembered their bargain, His rape of her, and His treachery.

She had remembered Reginald Watkins, her most recent and last 'payment' to the Devil.

She had remembered Richard, her long-dead husband, source of her fortune after she had bludgeoned him to death; her first payment.

She had remembered the demon that had told her of the need to do battle with Simon Colvin; of the redemption which had been promised her, if she were successful in destroying him.

She had remembered her long convalescence in hospital, after Colvin had proved harder to dispose of than she had hoped and she had come off worse from their earliest encounters.

She had remembered her dearest Rose, and their timeless love for each other.

She had remembered the death of the perverted cabinet minister in Rosemary's brothel, at the hands of the first demons she had ever summoned.

She had remembered the deaths she had brought about, of all the other V.I.P.s over the years; of the Kennedys, of her regret at the death of Malcolm X; of so many others, so much more deserving; and of an innocent peer in the marquee at Tintagel, after which, regrets or not, there had been no turning back.

She had remembered the last demon she had ever summoned, again in an attempt to destroy Colvin, this time with his woman, and its failure to do so.

She had remembered the odious Mr. Frye, and the kidnapping of Colvin's brats; and now she had remembered his and his catamite's fittingly violent deaths at her hands.

⚹   ⚹   ⚹

All this she remembers.

Lastly, she remembers, now that it is all over, the final death she had ever been the cause of, at Stonehenge.

Still she sits. Still she waits…

CHAPTER FIFTEEN

(Yet Another, Further, Different Tuesday)

"Y OU'RE NOT GOING, and that's final!" shouted Simon Colvin, at Cathy Beauchamp.

She turned from where she sat in their living room towards Dylan the angel, who stood by the sliding doors; a reversal of his and Colvin's positions from the previous day.

"Dylan, *tell him*, please, that he can't do this by himself. He needs me. He needs *us*."

"I cannot say that, Cathy, because it is not so. I already told you both yesterday that Simon has to meet the woman alone tonight."

"But he *can't*. That's not fair. We have to help him if we can."

"I can't help him," said the angel, "any more than I already have. Assuming the woman will want to exchange the children for the sword, only Simon can decide what to do when that time comes. It is neither for you nor I — even if I could — to interfere. Plus, there is likely to be great danger in what is about to take place. You should not be put at risk."

"All the more reason why I *should* be there!" She was emphatic, and looked again at Simon sitting opposite her. "*Please*, darling. I *must* come with you."

Colvin looked sorrowful, already regretting his recent outburst, but was nonetheless resolute. "Look, we've been around and around this a dozen times, in as many different ways. If you come with me,

I'll have to worry about you as well as the kids, and I'm going to need all my concentration if I'm to get them back without relinquishing the sword… though who on Earth — or anywhere else, for that matter — knows how I'm going to achieve both…?"

"Simon, I…"

"Cathy! I can't look after myself, them, *and* you. Accept it, *please.*"

Her earlier defiance was wavering, being replaced by a sullen resignation. "Well…"

"Well, nothing! I love you, Cathy, you know I do, and I want you to be here for me when I get back, whatever else happens. I'll need you then."

"*If* you get back." She was not yet beyond a little more emotional blackmail.

"*When.* I'm going to succeed. I have to."

"Okay, okay, I'm convinced. I see there's no arguing with the two of you." She smiled then, and relaxed from her rigidly rebellious pose into a calmer, less challenging one. "I love *you,* darling, you know that too. I'll always be there for you." She sighed, and shrugged. "Brunch, anyone?"

Dylan declined, as he always had, but she reheated some leftover pasta for herself and Simon which they ate while the three of them continued to talk over recent events.

"Do we have any idea who the two bodies were at that warehouse?" Simon asked of the angel.

"None, really. We think that the man had some connection with your adversary, did some work for her at times, but we've no idea who the boy was. We can only assume they were killed by the woman, but why, again, is anybody's guess. The beds were presumably for your children. They and the woman are no doubt en route to Stonehenge now, if they're not there already."

"Well, there were certainly no signs of life at her house," said Cathy, who had had to restrain Simon from attempting to break-and-enter the property, insisting that he would be of no use to anyone if he got himself arrested and locked up.

He had agreed reluctantly, and only after Dylan's assurances that there were no detectable psychic traces of either the woman or her young hostages; that they were long gone.

These three then left Eaton Square too, and headed back to the townhouse where the angel imposed a deep, revivifying, dreamless sleep upon Colvin (who had tried very hard to resist the idea), explaining that Simon would need all of his strength for any fight with the woman.

Dylan had left Cathy, and her slumbering lover, promising to return the following day with as much news as he could gather.

Now they sat and discussed what little — all but nothing — he had managed to learn.

Colvin felt better for his rest, but was still adamant that he had not needed it.

"You'll want every last reserve of your energies," insisted the angel. "You saw what the woman did to those other two. She has almost superhuman strength now."

"And she could be anywhere?" asked Cathy.

"Absolutely anywhere, except that she has to be able to reach Stonehenge tonight. Whatever power she wields that cloaks their whereabouts, it's impenetrable by any means we have at our disposal."

"That's a point. Just how is she going to get there? Not to Salisbury, I mean, but into Stonehenge tonight, after it's closed, and presumably into the stones' area? That's out of bounds too, roped off, even when it's open."

"I don't think we're in any doubt of her ability to incapacitate security guards or other measures they have there, are we?" Dylan looked at Simon. "You are going to have to find a way in, just as she is, although I'd suggest you wait for her to do whatever she has in mind first. It'll make your own entry all the easier. When do you plan to leave?"

"Shortly, I think. It's going to take a couple of hours to get there, and to be honest I want to see the place first. Not only to check out the lie of the land, but also because I've never actually been. I always wanted to, but just didn't ever get around to it."

"Oh, it's great. You'll love it," said Cathy, suddenly excited. "Somewhat smaller than most people expect, but a wonderful — what shall I call it? — auraful experience…" She stopped then, and grinned a little sheepishly. "Listen to me. Enthusing like I'm recommending somewhere to go on holiday. Not somewhere you may never come back from…" Her eyes betrayed a mixture of sadness and fear, which she tried to disguise by gathering up their dishes and clearing them away to the kitchen.

When she came back in and sat down again, Simon reached across and squeezed her hand slightly, reassuringly. He stroked her hair, noticing within it every imaginable red; it never ceased to amaze him that her hair rarely seemed quite the same shade twice.

He was also surprised at how little fear he felt, now that he was about to set off, and he put this down to the need to get the children back taking priority over all else. "I'll be fine. Everything will be fine. You wait and see."

Cathy nodded, and smiled.

He looked at his watch, and began preparing to leave.

The car journey along the M3 motorway, and then the A303 towards Salisbury, was uneventful and gave Simon Colvin much time for reflection.

The sword, which Dylan had now told them was believed to be an incarnation of the Holy Grail — something which meant little to him but seemed to make a great deal of sense to Cathy — lay quiescently behind him on the back seat, wrapped in a cloth.

Cathy had refused to come down to see him off, and so Dylan had done so, with the not altogether encouraging parting words, "I'll be watching."

His thoughts as he drove turned firstly to Elspeth. Poor, frantic Elspeth. He had hated lying to her, these past few days, but what choice had he? She could never know the truth. He still loved her, he knew. He probably always would, even if he couldn't live with her. (This did not conflict with his love for Cathy, which somehow had a different quality to it.) Perhaps one would always have a special bond with, an attachment for, a person with whom one had created new lives.

He remembered, then, the faces of his children on the day he had left them and, as always happened when this image came to mind, his eyes sprang with tears and a sharp, bitter ache knotted his insides. Driving through this bleary image was not a wise move, and he forced himself to think of something else.

He recalled chatting to Dylan on the banks of the Serpentine, telling him some of what had happened since leaving Elspeth and the children (this was not so distant from his previous recollection, of actually leaving them, but was far enough not to jeopardise his driving).

He had told the angel of the anguish he had gone through, immediately after the split. "Everything I've done," he had said, "leaving my wife and kids, and so on, seems wrong. Morally wrong, socially wrong, in *every* way wrong. But if I had chosen to stay, or to go back, for that reason alone, and spent the rest of my life wondering 'What would've happened if…?', then what kind of a life would that be?"

"A normal one?" suggested the angel.

That had been a turning point for Colvin, one at which he resolved to get on with living his new life and stop brooding over the old. (He was not always successful in this, far from it; but it had helped.) So many people, he realised — too many — spent their lives regretting something they did when they shouldn't have, or something they should have done when they didn't. Life, he had decided, was too short for such regrets.

Leaving the motorway for the A-road, his thoughts turned to the glimpse he had been given of Heaven, and the feeling of… wholeness… with which it had imbued him, albeit briefly. He thought of how thoroughly his life had changed over the last year, how readily he had come to accept things which seemed impossible; which he would previously have condemned as lunatic ravings from anybody else. What of the woman he had met there, who claimed to have no name, whom he had chosen to call 'Ellie'? Who was she, really? *What* was she? He would probably never know.

He thought, then, of Limbo, that endlessly grey plain of nothingness. Whatever came about as a result of this day's events, he hoped it was not his fate to spend eternity there. Surely even Hell would be preferable? Or would it?

Realising he was getting rather unhelpfully depressed now, he considered instead his relationship with Cathy. Beautiful, vibrant Catherine Beauchamp; as much light relief from his currently morbid thoughts as she had been from his daily life as a whole. For the first time in months, he wondered idly how her tax inspection was going, and this made him smile. He had, needless to say, had to remove himself from involvement in the investigation, after they became an 'item'. He loved Cathy unreservedly (he knew no other way to love); hoped more than anything to return to her safely, and with his children.

What on Earth would he tell Elspeth if the kids were to... but enough of that...

Then there was the woman herself, his adversary. He knew virtually nothing about her. Had she always been in league with these forces of evil? If not, what could possibly have happened in her past to make her serve them now? What must it be like, *really* like, to live for hundreds of years, to grow forever older without dying?

The car's cassette player stopped, and he ejected the tape and flipped it over, reinserting it to play the second side of *Woodstock Diary* (which had seemed a fitting choice, he felt). He might just get to the end of Side Two before arriving in Salisbury.

Already at Salisbury Plain, a very elderly, white-haired woman, carrying nothing but a small black clutch-bag, showed two young children around the ancient monoliths collectively known as Stonehenge.

She was surprised to discover, not having been there since the early 1970s, that access to the stones themselves was now prohibited (which only heightened her impression of the site's ever-diminishing size). This pathetic additional fencing, barely a guide-rope, would not make her job any harder.

She pointed out to the children, at this enforced distance, the inner circle of smaller bluestones, dwarfed by the great sandstone sarsens which ringed them. She told them mystical tales, of a race of giants once thought to have brought the stones all the way from Africa; legends of King Arthur, all connected with the henge, and Sarah innocently repeated everything they had learned of him during their recent trip to Tintagel. Had she ever been there? asked Sam. "Once," the woman said.

The children listened to other details as they walked around, on audio-commentary 'phones, but they much preferred the stories their daddy's friend told them. She was a nice old lady.

Simon Colvin thought better of stopping in Stonehenge's own car park, feeling that one lone vehicle's presence there after everyone else left would draw unwanted attention. Instead he parked at a Salisbury hotel where he had also eaten a late lunch before taking a taxi out to the henge. It was three o'clock when he arrived. There were four hours to go until the site closed; another nine before midnight.

His first impressions were, as Cathy had predicted, of how small the place was; that, and astonishment at how close the busy road came to such an historic (*if not particularly monumental*) monument.

Nevertheless, he was duly overwhelmed by the genuine sense of awe the henge inspired, as he took the tour around it, unaware that he had missed the woman's and his children's departure by a matter of minutes. By a similarly odd coincidence, they now rested in the very hotel at which his car was parked, although none of them spotted it there.

Simon Colvin was the last member of the public to leave Stonehenge, at a little after seven; he returned to the hotel, and there ate another hearty meal, surprised at how calm and ready he felt, given what was about to take place.

Once again though, he had no idea how close he came to those he so desperately needed to save, as they and the woman passed by the dining-room doors and left the hotel at a little before ten o'clock, just as he was breaking into the caramelised crust of a particularly tasty *crème brûlée*.

It was time. Time to put an end to it all.

Chapter Sixteen (The Battle For Everything)

SIMON COLVIN GOT stiffly up from his dining chair, having long since finished his meal, and left the hotel, going first to his car to retrieve the sword, still wrapped in its cloth, before hailing another taxi. It was half past eleven.

The driver was one of those who has seen everything in his day, and was not at all disinclined to regale passengers with tales of his past. It did not surprise him in the least that his latest fare wanted to go to the henge so long after it had closed. That was the second time this evening; the old woman with those two dumb kids being the first, a couple of hours before. There was obviously going to be some sort of illegal shindig or other nearby. It happened on occasion.

Colvin had hummed his way through the whole journey, partly to block out the drone of the driver, but also because the sword in his arms had begun to vibrate and make a few preliminary mumblings of its own, which increased the nearer they got to the site.

Again he thought it prudent to stop short of Stonehenge's car park, and asked the driver to pull up at the main intersection a few hundred yards from the entrance.

It occurred to Colvin that he had not considered any means of returning to Salisbury, once this was all over; he had not thought that far ahead.

Getting out of the taxi and paying his fare, he looked up at the sky immediately above the stones; it had turned, he thought, the colour of rotten honey (*can honey rot?*). Either way, it was a sure sign of the woman's presence there; her predilection for dramatic weather conditions to accompany her sorcery.

"Bloody 'ippies!" said the taxi driver, as he began to pull away. "Lightin' fires again. The council'll 'ave yer guts f'garters."

Colvin realised he had no idea of how to actually enter the site, nor of what he should do once he had got in, and the first probing fingers of fear and uncertainty began to press on him, chilling his spine and threatening to root him to the spot, unable to proceed at all.

The sword in his arms, though, jogged his focus back to matters at hand, as it shook itself free of the cloth and shone gold again, at full, near-blinding strength. It sang out, almost joyously, and the smell of roses which always seemed intrinsic to this display was nearly overpowering.

He began to walk slowly up and around the perimeter of the site, trying to keep below the line of the stones but still looking for a way in through the chain-link fencing. Not long after setting off, keeping to the farther, car-park side of the road, the sword suddenly twisted in his hand and somehow drew his eyes to a point at which the fence on the other side had been rent asunder, melted, the tips of its severed links still glowing red-hot.

He passed carefully through this opening and made his way towards the famous heelstone, standing on its own nearby, from the shadow of which he hoped to spy the woman, his children, or more likely all three, somewhere within the stone rings. To his right, he spotted the prostrate form of a security guard, apparently unconscious rather than slain. He assumed there would be others elsewhere, all similarly prone.

The eery, unnaturally shifting luminescence above him offered more than enough light to see by, but its peculiarly rolling (*Spielbergian?*) cloud formations — which seemed to fold in and out of themselves, growing and shrinking without ever leaving the confines of an area directly above the megalithic circle — kept shifting his sense of perspective. Stones which seemed huge, close by and brightly lit one second were the very next minuscule, far away and plunged into impenetrable blackness. Any movement therein, human or otherwise, could be real or illusory; he would not be able to tell which until he, too, entered the great stone henge.

Whilst he knew not what to expect once he stepped forth, he did know that he *was* expected, and saw no further point in subterfuge. That said, there was also no logic in walking into a trap either, and so he moved from cover, dropping down into a shallow ditch and creeping clockwise around it to the other side; to the point at which the outer ring was mostly comprised of fallen stones. He was now directly opposite the vast wall of complete, lintelled sarsens and the single heelstone beyond. He had no element of surprise from here, but neither did the woman.

As soon as he passed between the first two toppled monoliths — felled giants — into the circle itself, a harsh wind picked up all around him, soughing temptingly through the stones and beckoning him with indistinct voices — his own and others' — tugging at him with blustering breeze and words alike: *to the devil damned damn the woman i love her in the body it's a harp how much more of this can i take what on earth am i doing blood and souls wings oh well in for a penny trippin' eternity...*

He stopped, listened, and then thought it better not to. He moved on, towards the middle of the ring, but the voices were not going to let him off that easily: *visitation your anger scares me odd is a very good word for it guilt oh simon please don't go everywhere nowhere anywhere if only they knew...*

He reached the centre of the great site, and stood next to the so-called altar stone. There was still no sign of the woman or his children; only the relentless, talking wind: *friend end of test he's ready pity darling simon simon simon the last time whatever happens daddy daddy...*

The sound of his children's voices made him pay attention, scanning all around for a glimpse of them, hoping that it had been their real calls he heard, and not just another current of warm, deceiving air. Nothing.

There was nowhere else to go. He glanced at his watch, the time just visible in the leaping radiance from above. One minute to midnight: *five days do you have it look fuck you dylan do you know where they are an odd venture oh jesus fucking christ oh god no did you touch her...*

"Do you know where they are?" He startled himself, speaking aloud without realising it, something he had heard in the breeze.

"They are here, Colvin."

It was her.

He peered into the flickering half-light, even held up his brilliant sword in order to see better, desperate to locate her, but could not tell from which direction the voice had come. It seemed all around him, but he was sure this time that it was not just a sound in the wind.

"They are here." This time it was in his ear, as if she stood right next to him. He spun around, through three hundred and sixty degrees. Still nothing. "They are here." Far away now. So distant as to be beyond the stones. "Here."

He spotted her now. The woman. The children were nowhere to be seen. He sought them, but they remained hidden. She seemed to be strolling, meandering along the edges of the stones, the great wall of sarsens; she was peering upward all the while, as if at something high above the giant uprights, in the clouds.

"Where are my children?" he cried, over the noises of the breeze — more natural now, less voice-laden — and of the sword.

"They are here." Almost reluctantly, she began to leave the shade of the sarsens, and walked more purposefully towards him.

"Show them to me. Show me they're safe."

"They are not harmed. Not yet."

"Touch my children, bitch, and I'll kill you!" He brandished the glowing weapon in the direction of her approach.

"So you say. You cannot kill me, little man. Not you, and not that glorified bodkin there."

"Don't come any closer." He was not sure what he would do if she did; and indeed she did. He was suddenly aware that he had no actual idea of how to sword-fight. His confidence before her bravura was wavering.

She laughed at him. "We have things to discuss, you and I. Things to do, before I destroy you."

He was still certain that the sword was far more important to them both than she made out, and he resolved to use it wisely in his bargaining for the children's lives. Even if he were to die, he had to make sure they lived. Dylan, whom he hoped was watching the proceedings as promised, would get them back to Elspeth. He had to make a stand, a show of defiance.

"What," he jeered, "no demons to aid you this time, woman? No unhuman allies to do your bidding for you?"

"None. I have no need of any. I have something else, something entirely more fitting, in store for you." She was close to him now, and they had begun to move around the altar stone, keeping it between them. "Can you guess what it might be?"

"I know that you want this sword. And I know that I want my children back. If you're ready to, let's bargain. Let's to business."

Her eyes showed a flickering trace of emotion as he said that, although he could not define exactly what it was she had revealed. Just as soon, it was gone from her face and her manner. She laughed again, cruelly.

"You think we are here to conduct an exchange? Oh, what a foolish little man you are. I have no need to bargain with the likes of you."

He was puzzled now. "Then what *are* we here for?"

"Why, to destroy you, of course. What else?"

Fear gripped him. What was he to do now? He had a weapon, true, but she had the strength of many. Was it to come down to a simple matter of hand-to-hand combat? Hardly one of his strengths. Thinking they would need as clear a space as possible in which to fight, if fight they must, he backed away from the altar stone, out into the widest point between stones, waiting for her to follow. Instead, with one lightning-quick movement she was atop the altar stone itself, hands on hips, looking down on him.

"Retreating, little man?"

"No. Getting ready to fight you. Come here."

That laugh again. "*Me?* Cross swords with *you?* Come, now, what do you take me for? I have other plans for you. I've told you that already. And I will even give you a chance at besting me, if you think you can."

He listened intently, hopeful now, awaiting an explanation. None was forthcoming. She simply raised her hands to her mouth and called out: "Come, children." She smiled, evilly, between her cupped fingers. "Come to Daddy."

There they were, one to each side of the great wall of stone, Sarah on the right, little Sam to the left. They moved stiffly, awkwardly, their arms behind their backs, out onto the grassy clear area towards their father. When they got to within a few feet — Colvin hadn't moved, not knowing to which of them he should run first, wanting to grab and hold on to them both — he saw their faces; their vacant expressions, punctuated with white, irisless orbs instead of eyes. The children stopped dead, and stared at — through — their father from out of those sightless sockets.

"What..." he croaked, "what have you done to them?"

The woman, from her position high on the altar stone, had a wholly self-satisfied air about her; already one of triumph. "You wanted a bargain. Let us have one, but on my terms. You people, you... mortals... hold such store by love. 'Love conquers all', you like to think. Well, let's put that to the test, shall we? Let us test that love.

"You want to kill me, Colvin, don't you? You said as much. Well, you can do so; you can win. All you have to do is kill your children. Destroy them — kill something you love so dearly — and I, too, shall be destroyed. You will have won."

"You must be mad!"

"I do not think that is in any doubt, is it? Could you have lived as long as I, in the way that I have, and remained sane?"

He ignored her; had no time for pity. "I will not kill my children, not for anything."

"No? Not even when they wish to extinguish you?"

"What do you mean?"

"I have — how shall I put this, that one so simple-minded might understand? — I have altered them, possessed them. I have imbued them with a little of my strength, and a few other quite pleasing... characteristics. Smile for your daddy, children."

He forced himself to look at his loved ones' blank, blind faces, as their lips parted to reveal teeth that could never have been theirs; could never have been human. Long they were, and needle-sharp; blackened, and ugly, and vicious. Their hands came around from behind their backs, and were gnarled talons that clicked and clacked together as the children stood gazing hungrily in their father's direction. They began to drool, a stinking, discoloured bile, as the woman continued:

"I told you before that they were not harmed. That is not strictly true. They suffer, you see, some discomfort in their current form, and they have been... *persuaded*... that their torment ends only after they have destroyed you. This blindness of theirs is an unfortunate by-product of the sorcery involved. But they don't need to see you to find you. They can sniff you out. They smell your fear. And they look very keen, don't you think?"

"*Fuck you!*" This simple, uninventive retort hardly seemed appropriate, but there was little else he could say. He looked; his children were hurting, and he could think of nothing to do that would help ease their pain.

The woman seemed to have anticipated his reaction. "Would you put an end to all this, Colvin? Would you save your little brats?"

He cared for little else, now. The sword meant nothing to him. Armageddon meant nothing to him. Only his children. "Tell me how," he pleaded.

"It is a very simple alternative, really. Give me the sword, and I will let them live. I shall still have to kill you, of course, because I must, but I will restore them to their previous forms. I will even return them to their mother for you. Give me the sword, and they shall live."

He looked down at the mystical weapon in his hands. It was strangely, surprisingly quiet, as if it knew that its fate was in the balance; depended upon Colvin's decision.

He had told Dylan that if it came down to a simple choice, between the sword and his children, he would let the weapon go. Now that choice had to be made, but one thing stayed his hand; stopped him from hurling the sword to the woman's feet and surrendering his life for theirs.

"If I give you this," he said, struggling with every bitter word, "you will kill me, and my children will live. Correct?"

"I have said so."

"And you will win."

"I will."

"Then they would have to live in... in a Hell on Earth. Would I wish that for them? I think not."

"A Hell on Earth would not be so very bad..." she began, but she clearly wavered, had not expected resistance.

"I've been told otherwise."

"Then they shall have you!" she screamed in furious, frustrated rage, and before he knew what was happening his own children had leapt upon him, tore at him with scalpel claws, gnashed at him with razor teeth.

He pushed them back from him, and flesh came away in their jaws, in their fingers.

He turned to run, and stumbled forwards, falling flat. In a second the children were on his back, inflicting small but deep wounds wherever their hands and mouths fell. He rolled over, and felt their tiny bodies under his. He was both desperate to escape them and terrified that he might crush them; might hurt them. He could not fight his own children.

He shuffled backwards away from them again, and stood. They spread out and began to circle him, one on each side, a few feet away. He swung the sword around vaguely, half-heartedly, trying to keep them at a distance but afraid of touching them with its knife-edged blade. They dodged in and out of its range, feinting with their bodies just as he did with the weapon in his hands. Blood coursed from a dozen different wounds on him, but he was barely aware of their existence. They stung, distantly, but he had no time for pain.

From her position atop the altar stone, the woman laughed as Colvin frantically tried to evade his children's attacks. She encouraged their efforts, urged them on, and they willingly obliged.

He tried to make his way back around to the altar stone again, and to the woman, hoping to get to her without harming or being further harmed by his children. When they got too close, he tried to slap at them, brush them aside, with the flat of the sword's blade, but he found even this gentle counterattack all but impossible to maintain.

He approached the stone, and swung the weapon high across it, at the woman's legs. One second she was there, the next she was gone; and the next, back again as if she had never left the spot. If she had jumped high and clear, as he suspected, then it was faster than his eye could see. He did not believe she could vanish and reappear at will, or she would surely have done so before.

Her speed in dodging his swipe demoralised him almost as much as having to evade his own children, but he was still able to appreciate the cunning she had employed in conducting this final battle in such a way. Whichever way it ended, he lost.

He tried to turn the sword in his hand, and bring it down in an arc from which she could not leap away, but his legs were suddenly grabbed from behind and he fell forwards, banging his head hard against the side of the stone. Dazed, briefly unable to move at all, he registered the sensations almost detachedly as his children fed off him, ripped the flesh from his limbs and tasted him.

As he felt his life-stuff seep from him, and death begin to envelope his mind, in a bloody mess beneath them he pleaded with them to stop, told them he loved them, and still they tugged and clawed and chewed at him.

The only feeling he had left, anywhere, was of the sword in his hand, and with one last feeble effort before he lost all consciousness he rolled over and swung it wildly around him. He heard screaming; the screaming of his own children, and this jerked him violently back to full awareness. He looked through eyes into which blood poured from a gaping wound on his forehead and saw the children standing back away from him, both nursing gashes — Sarah's in her thigh, little Sam's in his upper arm — injuries he had inflicted upon them.

He wept, and begged them to forgive him. They warily kept their distance from him, and showed no signs of recognition even that he was their father, only that his demise would ease their suffering.

He would not kill them, he knew. He seemed unable to destroy the woman, who still laughed from on high, leering down at his ruined body, sensing her imminent victory. He looked up from where he lay at the base of the altar stone, and saw the peculiar glowing clouds roiling chaotically above them. These were but one small representation of what the world could expect if Hell came to rule over it. He could not let that happen, either. If he could not kill his children, or the woman, then he would have to flee them, escape to fight another day.

He struggled to his feet, and now all feeling returned as his body blazed with a thousand tiny agonies. He pushed himself off, away from the stone, and ran straight between the two children, heading for the vast wall of sarsen stones.

"Get him!" screeched the woman, and the children gave chase.

It seemed to take an age to reach the stones. With every panicked step he took towards them, they appeared more distant. A trick of the shifting light perhaps, or of the woman, but eventually he reached their shelter and turned to see how close were his pursuers. The children were almost upon him again. He had no strength left for further flight. Knowing that he could not actually use it against them, he still raised the sword up in front of himself, pointed it back towards the woman on the altar stone.

"Simon." A voice, to his side, from behind one of the stones; he half turned his head towards its source. There was Cathy. She moved in front of him, and then walked forward and impaled herself upon his sword. He tried to withdraw the blade, but it was impossible. A sensation unlike any other he had ever known — gentle, warm, pleasant — flowed into him through the weapon. He looked into Cathy's face. She tried to smile at him, but blood welled up out of her mouth and trickled down her chin. It was hard to tell if her lips moved at all, but he thought he heard her whisper, *"His will be done."* Her eyes closed. So she died. Upright. Proud. Impaled upon a sword her lover could not even discard.

As if from a great distance — much farther away than the altar stone — he heard the woman's bellow: *"NO!"*

Then a huge, ferocious gale blew up around them all. A mighty noise roared in his ears. On the end of the sword, his dead lover's hair blew about her head, a bright, pre-Raphaelite mane, giving her terribly slain form a brief semblance of life, as from the end of the sword, protruding from her back, a stream of flaming, blazing light poured out in the direction of the altar stone. It struck the woman in exactly the same place on her body that the blade had entered Cathy's. It exited her back similarly, and danced around the fallen stones behind her, seeming to take on flickering, indistinct shapes.

The woman writhed in agony, pierced through and held upright by this beam. Parts of her seemed to burst outwards, folds of torn flesh hanging from chalk-white bones; others seemed to implode, leaving gaping holes within her. She warped. She deformed. Gradually, she began to wither and disintegrate, turning to dust within her clothes. As she lost all recognisable human substance, so the light from the sword gathered stability and direction, and as Colvin watched, unable to do anything else, the rays moved, spread out and fell into position, re-creating in a lattice of brilliance the original architecture of Stonehenge. Wherever a monolith had once stood, but now was missing, so its outline reappeared in shining precision until they were surrounded by an entire, breathtaking temple of light.

Despite all that had happened, Colvin could not help but stare in unparalleled wonder at this display. He did not even notice the last moments of the woman's existence on Earth, until her empty clothing fell to the surface of the altar stone and cut off the streaming flow of rays from the sword's bloody tip. As this ceased, he was able at last to lower the weapon, and Cathy slid from it to land lifeless upon the grass. He dropped the sword to the ground as he heard two other voices cry out simultaneously: *"Daddy! Daddy!"*

From each side of him, his children ran into his arms, crying natural tears from fully restored, sighted eyes. He held them at arms' length, and examined them. Apart from the small wounds he had inflicted, which it stung him to see, they were both back to normal. They showed no signs of recalling their recent ordeal; no memories of their possession. He wept too, then, tears of inexpressible joy, and hugged them back close into his body, feeling their wholesome warmth, sharing and absorbing their vitality.

Looking about him, he noticed that the intricate web of light still encircled them, thrumming with a vibrant life all of its own. Then he glanced down, saw Cathy again, and kneeled by her, cradled her head in his lap, brushed hair back from her brow. The children stood beside him, but were now staring in awe at the dazzling display around them, seemingly unaware of their father's distress as he wept again, in all-consuming sorrow this time, for the loss of his lover.

It might have been minutes. It might have been hours. Simon Colvin had no concept of passing time as he held on to Cathy, trying to hug his warmth into her, to stop the inevitable chilling of her body. He had stopped crying. He had no tears left to cry.

Shivering in a sudden cool breeze, he looked up to see his children gambolling among the light sculptures which still shone all about them.

Whenever they ran, unharmed, through a beam, it broke apart into rainbow shards, as if from a prism, and then re-formed as it was left for another. The children were laughing, and he could not help but smile, tiredly, at their innocent antics. They seemed oblivious of all that had gone on, and he was determined to keep them that way. He would have to move Cathy for the moment, perhaps to her own car if it was here, whilst he took the children to a place of safety, presumably back to his hotel. Wearily taking hold of her body, behind neck and knees, he made to stand.

There was a tap on his shoulder, and he jerked his head up to see a young man who could only be described as nothing less than beautiful, with stunningly bright blue eyes. It took a while to register who stood before him. "Dylan?"

"Yes, Simon, it's me. You've won."

"Have I?" He looked again at Cathy, in his arms, and was not so sure. Reluctantly, he released her body again, gently back onto the grass, and stood.

"As the woman said to you," explained the angel, "kill something you love dearly, and she herself would be destroyed. Cathy followed you here, watched what was happening — as did I — knew you could not kill your children, and she did the one thing she could to help you. It was all she ever wanted to do; to help."

Colvin struggled for words, a half formed recollection: "You... you told me... told us... the sword couldn't help someone take their own life. You lied."

"I didn't lie, Simon. I cannot. But it seems I was wrong."

"Bring her back."

"What do you mean?"

"I mean, bring her back to life. You're an angel. You can do anything. Bring her back to me, Dylan, *please*."

"I can't do that."

"But you *must*."

There were tears, now, in the angel's eyes, as he looked at his friend, witnessed his grief. "I cannot. It's not that I won't or mustn't, Simon. I *can't*. I don't know how."

"But I do." A voice, to their side, from behind another of the stones;

there was a small, plain-looking woman, wearing a loose-fitting, rather drab robe. It was the woman Colvin had met, who had shown him Heaven.

She walked forward, and picked up the sword, moving with it towards Cathy's body. Colvin yelled "NO!", and went to lash out at her as she plunged the weapon back into the original wound, but he was restrained by Dylan — could do nothing but watch as the surrounding beams, the stones of light, moved again, grew agitated and then flowed outwards and upwards, into the now clear, dark, starry night sky, where they danced and wove themselves in and out of complex geometrical patterns before suddenly spearing earthwards and pouring back into the sword; into the end of its hilt. There was a single, blinding flash, and when Colvin could see again, there were no more rays of light, there was no sword, and there was no longer a gaping hole through his lover's body.

When Cathy's eyes reopened, Dylan released his grip on Simon and allowed him to run to her. Smothering her with kisses, Colvin held her head in his hands, framing her face, while she tried to say something which he had to strain to hear: "I love you," she sighed.

Together they looked up at their two angelic allies. Dylan grinned — ever the Cheshire Cat — obviously pleased with the outcome of events, while the other spoke to them. "Thank you, Simon. Thank you both."

"You're welcome," he said, as his children returned and tugged at their father's sleeve, demanding a share of his attentions, "and thank you."

"You're welcome. Now, there is one more thing that needs to be done."

Colvin had never felt so tired. "What now? Haven't I... we... done enough?"

"Yes, Simon, you have. More than enough. This is for someone else to do. I must go now. Come, Dylan."

"Yes, ma'am. Simon, Cathy, it's been... well, it's been a gas, dudes."

"So long, Dylan." Colvin turned to the heavenly woman, as he held tightly to Cathy with one arm and to his children with the other. "One last thing. What is your real name?"

"I told you before, Simon, I have no name. You may know of my brother, though. Well, my half-brother, really. Not many people realise that God had a daughter, too…"

… with which she, and Dylan, disappeared.

REMINISCENCE (8)

S HE HAS REMEMBERED SO very much. Too much.

She has sat. She has waited.

Now the waiting is over.

Epilogue (2001 a.d.)

THE ROOM IN which she has been waiting is virtually bare — just the chair she sits upon and a small, almost featureless table. Neither of the doors opposite her has opened since she arrived.

She has no idea of how long she has been waiting. A few minutes? An hour? Days? A lifetime?

Her last earthly recollections are the death of Simon Colvin's woman at Stonehenge, a brilliant light pouring outwards, and a sharp, stabbing pain. A vague memory of greater agony. Then nothing more.

Now a door opens, and the Devil enters.

He looks no different from the last time she saw Him, so many years before. He is even dressed identically. He is still beautiful.

He smiles, as disarmingly as ever, and speaks in the same smooth, seductive tones: "You have failed Me."

His eyes — deepest blue; mauve even — moist; not quite tearful — full of infinite intelligence, passion, sorrow — bore into her, penetrate her.

"I know." She can only agree. She knows what to expect, but the prospect of an eternity in Hell holds very little fear for her now. She has never felt so weary. She just wants it all to be over, but will not give Him the satisfaction of seeing her in defeat and so manages to adopt a conversational tone: "You have changed little, since we last met."

"As have you," says He.

She laughs out loud, derisively. "Come, now, that is a long way from the truth. Even *your* deceptions cannot stretch reality that far."

"But I do not lie. Look —" He produces, with a mere sweep of His hand, a full-length mirror which hangs in mid-air before her — "stand up, and see for yourself."

She does so, and reflected there is a naked young woman, with deep blue eyes, smooth, pale skin and lustrous, raven hair worn loose to below the shoulders. She is very beautiful, this woman, and it takes her a while to recognise herself in the mirror; herself as she was before she ever made a pact with the creature standing opposite.

She looks down then, at her own blemished, wrinkled, ancient hands. She is also still fully clothed. She grabs a handful of hair and pulls it into view; it is frosty white, lank and lifeless. She sighs, and sits back down. "More treachery?"

"But of course. You cannot possibly expect Me to give you the pleasure of appearing to yourself as you now look to others; as you once looked to all. There are all manner of torments awaiting you, and all manner of tormentors, many of whom demand youthful flesh from their playthings. I can hardly deny them that, can I?"

"Some things never change, I see." She still refuses to reveal the greater terror that has begun to gnaw at her.

"Not in Hell."

She tires of these word-games. "So, what happens now?"

"I take you there. You come with Me, to Hell."

She smiles — surprised that she is able to, in the face of all that awaits her — "Before we go, I have something to give you."

"You do?" He seems genuinely intrigued.

She reaches into her black clutch-bag, and produces from it a small revolver.

"What have we here," asks the Devil, "a child's toy?"

Without another word, she raises the pistol in both hands, and aims it at His beautiful head.

He laughs.

"Come, now, do you really think bullets can harm Me?"

"Not any ordinary bullets, no."

"Ah, I see. What are they then, silver? You think you confront some moon-crazed werewolf?" His laughter continues, but stops abruptly as she speaks again.

"Silver is not the metal used for these bullets."

There is a brief red flicker of irritation in His eyes. "Enough of this! Come with Me now…"

"There was just enough of the Grail left," says she, "to fill all six chambers."

"*The Grail?*" Perhaps for the first time ever, the Devil knows fear. His face clouds. "Such power is not yours to wield."

"And yet I have it here, in my hands. With it I can destroy *your* power."

He looks at the gun, pointed at His head. "You have no concept of My power; no knowledge of its true source."

"No? Perhaps a little bird told me. Or a little angel." She lowers the weapon slightly, until its sights are levelled at a point between the Devil's legs, at what must rest there between them.

"You… *you*… cannot destroy *Me*." Lucifer is unable to grasp the inconceivable. "I — I am eternal."

"Nothing is eternal." She fires.

He bellows: *"FATHER! PROTECT ME!"*, but this plea goes unheeded.

She fires again. Again. Again. Again. Again.

With each report, she whispers to herself, "Blood and souls. Blood and souls. Blood and souls…"

A great hole has opened up in the Devil. Ragged flesh surrounds it. No blood flows. His beauty dissolves before her, and He takes on His true form. It is impossible to behold, and she closes her eyes, but somehow still sees as the wound in Him widens further and turns to semi-liquid, begins to spiral, faster and faster. Spinning outwards from this central orifice, the Devil loses all shape, and grows in size, but not in mass, as He is dispersed in front of her. Some features remain — eyes, mouth, one elongated, imploring hand — and all protest, though they toss and jumble around in this near-gaseous tempest. Then, as if murky water pulled towards a drain, the great vortex sucks the Devil back into Himself; towards that hole, the point at which her bullets entered Him — the only static point in all this turmoil — until nothing is left but a mouth. All else has dissipated and disappeared.

"God!" it says, as it vanishes.

All is now still.

A door — the other door — opens and a small, plain-looking, green-eyed woman in her early thirties enters. She wears a loose-fitting, rather drab robe.

Still sitting, opposite the one who has just entered, the other speaks, dazedly. "Who are you?"

"I have no name."

"Then what should I call you?"

"Anything you wish."

"May I — may I call you Rosemary?" She has no real idea why she asks this.

"I prefer 'Rose'."

"Are you…?" She frowns.

"No, I am not her, but you may call me by her name."

"Thank you."

"I need to take you somewhere. I need you to come with me. I need you to trust me."

"Where are we going?"

"Heaven."

"Am I dead?" It seems the only thing to say.

"You are."

"Is it over? Is it all really, finally over?"

"It is. Come, sister. Shall we go to Heaven together?"

She has no doubts. "Yes."

They link arms. It is the first time they touch and a shock — neither pleasure nor pain — runs up both their arms and across their backs, gradually fading along the lengths of their spines. Each seems a little startled by this sensation, as they walk towards the door, which opens in front of them. They step through.

For the first time in nearly one hundred and fifty years, she weeps.

THE END